MERRY MIX-UPS

EMILY BYBEE

5 PRINCE PUBLISHING

Published by 5 PRINCE PUBLISHING & BOOKS, LLC

PO Box 865, Arvada, CO 80001

www.5PrinceBooks.com

ISBN digital: 978-1-63112-328-3

ISBN print: 978-1-63112-329-0

Cover Credit: Marianne Nowicki

4272023

THIS TITLE WAS PREVIOUSLY PUBLISHED IN THE 2022 A ROMANCE TO
REMEMBER ANTHOLOGY BY 5 PRINCE PUBLISHING

MERRY MIX-UPS

CHAPTER 1

MAX

COME OUT FOR DINNER THEY SAID. IT'LL BE FUN, THEY SAID. RIGHT before they dropped the bomb.

Blind dates and I didn't mix. The last one ended in expletives —some even I'd never heard. It's not like I care anyway. I'm not here to impress anyone.

I paused outside by the door. Ocean Aire was one of the most exclusive restaurants in downtown Denver. How Brad got reservations with two days' notice was another of his secrets. Especially this close to the holidays, the restaurant was probably booked at least a month out. I straightened my jacket and brushed snowflakes off the shoulders, then tucked in my shirt for the third time.

I'd have been much happier to be the third wheel, as usual. Brad's fiancée, Becca, loved to go to swanky places, and I ended up being the odd man out if they convinced me to come along— which wasn't often. But this time Becca pushed until I gave in. I should have known something was up.

Black smears on my hand caught my eye as I reached for the doorhandle. Damn, I thought I got it all. I pulled back and stepped to the side to hold the door and nodded to a couple in a suit and sparkly dress. I fit in like a square peg in a round hole.

The grease smudged the handkerchief I always carried, one of many habits my grandfather had passed down, along with the pride of being a third-generation firefighter. I scrubbed at my fingers for a minute before I accepted the fact that nothing would get all the evidence of my profession from my nail beds.

Stuffing the linen back in my coat pocket, I gritted my teeth. Brad had pulled the best friend card when I tried to back out of the evening, and said dinner was on him. I'd be sure to order extra drinks—the good stuff.

That was the least he could do for setting me up with Becca's college roommate, Cathy, or Carrie, or whatever her name was. All I knew were the stories Becca told us about her richer-than-shit-kleptomaniac friend—hysterical stories until you're expected to wine and dine the woman.

I wrapped my fingers around my wrist. The cold metal of the watch unknotted my stomach as I pressed on the clasp to be sure it was tight. I'd worn the watch every day since my grandfather passed away six months ago and left it to me, along with everything else he possessed.

With one last deep breath, I walked through the door. Warm air and the smell of fresh seafood washed over me. Expensive seafood. They probably charged a fee for breathing in the flipping scent.

Red poinsettias and twinkling lights covered every open surface of the place, but the last thing I felt was festive. More like going to my own funeral. I took off my jacket and folded it over my arm.

"Do you have a reservation?" The hostess smiled, her gaze lingering on my button-down shirt—one of two that I owned—which was a tad tight over my shoulders.

"It's under Mason. My friends are already here, I believe." My voice sounded odd—too formal, not me.

"Let me check your coat." She lifted it from my hands before I could say anything and slipped it on a hanger, then waved. "Right this way."

We weaved our way through the restaurant. Fine linen covered the tables and, by my judgement, expensive silverware and crystal graced the surfaces. Great idea, bring a kleptomaniac to a place with sparkly stuff to steal everywhere. And Brad, the architect, was supposed to be the smart one of the two of us.

The three sat in a curved booth toward the back of the dining area. Brad hopped from his seat when he spotted me. No escape now.

Becca beamed and waved me to the booth. "You're late," she scolded. "We were just about to call you."

I clapped a hand on Brad's back. "Sorry, had to clean up after work..." My gaze moved to the woman sitting next to Becca. I blinked, the rest of my sentence gone from my brain in a flash. The woman nodded in greeting and I remembered to close my gaping mouth.

Blonde waves fell over her shoulders and blue eyes gazed up from under her lashes. She'd be considered a knockout in any forum. But what stoked the embers in my chest to a raging flame was her smile. Something about her smile seemed so comforting.

"Max, this is Cassi, my roommate, back in the day."

"Nice to meet you," I managed. "I've heard a lot about you." Too bad you're probably going to steal anything that isn't nailed down.

CHAPTER 2

CASSI

Talk about an undersell. Becca described Brad's roommate as a stand-up guy. Which put my expectations of his looks at approximately zero.

Instead, I was faced with a guy who could have modeled for a sculpture of a Greek God, muscles and all. His dark hair was on the longish side, brushing the collar of his shirt. Then our eyes met, and I swore I felt like I was falling. I blinked and gripped the table to steady myself.

"So nice to meet you as well," I returned his greeting, hoping Becca had left out some of our more scandalous escapades from college.

Oh, yeah, she set me up to drool and look like an idiot. I kicked her under the table and darted a glare to her knowing face while Max slid into the booth beside me. His broad shoulders and muscular biceps strained at the seams of his white button-down. If it ripped open—I tore my thoughts away from what his back must look like—and met his gaze. Electrical shocks radiated through my torso. God, it's been a long dry spell, but geez.

"We ordered some appetizers while we were waiting on you," Brad said as he settled in and put an arm around Becca. She snuggled into him. They fit together like puzzle pieces. Even their names went together, Becca and Brad. How sickly sweet. I'd never been the jealous type, but seeing the two of them together, so in love, sent prickles of the emotion over my skin.

Their conversation—mostly Becca telling Brad how wonderful he was—gave me a moment to compose myself and I took a sip of water from the crystal wineglass.

"Well," Max said from beside me. "Since Brad's buying, let's get a round of drinks going."

His deep voice reverberated through my chest.

"I second that," I said, my voice coming out more cheerleader-esque than I'd planned. I cleared my throat.

Max signaled the waiter. "What do you have on tap?"

The waiter listed off a dozen microbrews, all local.

"Oh no," Brad said from across the table. "You're going to have to cheat on old reliable."

I furrowed my brow. "Old reliable?"

"Max here is, let's say, a simple man. Not a fan of micro-brews." Brad smirked and leveled his gaze at Max. "He's more of a Colorado Kool-Aid kind of guy."

"Nothing wrong with the silver bullet." Max's cheeks reddened, and he tugged at his collar.

"Yeah, if you can't handle real beer." Brad laughed.

"It's a local brewery too, ya know," Max answered.

"We'll be sure to have a cooler of Coors at the wedding just for you," Becca said, and elbowed Brad in the ribs.

I glanced at Max, then said to Becca, "I think Coors was all we drank in college."

Brad nodded to the waiter. "So, I'll have a top shelf dirty martini. My beautiful fiancée will have a Bailey's chocolate martini and give him whatever beer you have that's close to Coors."

"The Celestial lager would be as close as I can think," the waiter answered. "For you, miss?"

I opened my mouth to order the lager as well, not really into the swanky drinks.

"Oh, she'll have the same as me," Becca jumped in. "You have to try the martini. It's amazing."

The waiter nodded and strode away.

I chewed on the inside of my lip and picked up one of the many pieces of silverware in front of me, a small spoon. Becca and I had been friends forever, even before college. Of our four roommates, she was the only one I stayed in touch with. But she'd always been the boss.

Hairs raising on the back of my neck brought me out of my brooding. I glanced up to find Max eyeing me—and the spoon— and set it down. God, he probably thinks I'm a fidgety freak.

I rested my elbows on the tablecloth and gripped my hands together. When I looked up, I realized the new position put my face closer to Max, like I was leaning into him. Flinching, I pulled back to settle against the cushion and put my hands in my lap.

Max's eyes grew wide, and he glanced at my face, then to my purse where it sat on the bench next to me. I followed his gaze. The silver spoon and a small fork rested on the open zipper of my purse. I must have bumped them with my elbow.

Max leaned over to pluck the silverware up before they slipped further into my bag. "Uh, I think you dropped these."

"Oh, what a klutz." I grabbed the spoon and fork and put them back in perfect order with the rest of the utensils.

He cleared his throat but didn't comment further.

The waiter returned with our drinks and I downed half the martini without tasting it. Vodka burned my sinuses, and the alcohol warmed its way to my stomach. My empty stomach. Oh, this was strong. I grabbed the tiny garnish, a chocolate truffle, and slipped it off the miniature gold trident.

Warmth entered my bloodstream and flowed over my body. I'd been a lightweight in college, but now I was flat out pathetic. Drinking was not a part of my life these days, except on special occasions. Almost marrying an alcoholic can have that effect on a person. Not only did he steal five years of my life, but he'd also ruined drinking for me. Bastard.

His face flashed in my mind, and I downed the other half of the martini as if to prove to him I was still whole, capable of having fun. Blinking, I lifted my gaze to find the entire table's eyes on me.

"Someone's ready to get this party started." Brad signaled the waiter to bring me another.

"Oh, no," I tried to wave him off. "I'll just have water or—"

"Stop, we're celebrating!" Becca cut in, laughing. "Maybe try to taste the next one."

"What are we celebrating?" I asked, fiddling with the gold trident.

She rolled her eyes. "My engagement!" She paused and spoke as if an afterthought, "Plus, you moving back here, of course. And maybe now the four of us going out will be a regular thing."

Max chugged half his beer and waved to a passing server. "I'll need another of the Heavenly or whatever lagers."

Guess I'm not the only one with some nerves going on.

The appetizers arrived with my second drink that would only add to my full-blown buzz. The waiter cleared my empty glass and passed out small plates.

"Oh, here you go. Take this as well." Max plucked the gold trident from my still-fidgeting fingers and held it up for the waiter. "Don't want that falling into your purse."

I frowned. "Um, thank you?"

"No problem." He reached to fill his plate with tiny tacos, not touching the crab patties.

I munched on bread as I watched him. Was he avoiding eye contact? You're just paranoid. It's been too long since you went on a date.

I got up the nerve to speak. Maybe the vodka was helping a bit. "So, Max, do you work with Brad in his firm?"

"Oh, he's not an architect," Becca jumped in. "Not much for desk jobs and crunching numbers, right, Max?"

"Well, not all of us can be lawyers, Becca," Max answered in a tone that told me he wanted to roll his eyes. A dry chuckle huffed from his mouth. "Sorry to disappoint."

"Not at all. I didn't mean to assume…" I stumbled over my tongue.

"I didn't say there was anything wrong with being a firefighter," Becca exclaimed. "I just wouldn't want Brad to be running into burning buildings." She snuggled even closer into his side. Any closer and she'd be sitting on his lap.

I ignored Becca and focused on Max. "So, a firefighter. That's a really hard job."

He held out one hand over the white tablecloth. "Got the soot and grease to prove it."

His hands looked nearly raw from scrubbing, but a dark line had settled in the dry beds of his cuticles.

I swallowed another bite of bread. "Have you tried Working Balm?"

His brow furrowed, and he actually met my gaze.

"It's a cream," I rushed on. "My brother swears by it. He's an electrician."

"Really?" His voice held a dump truck full of doubt.

I glanced toward Becca. Everything I said seemed to be wrong. "Three brothers in the trades, actually." I tried for a joking tone. "If you need a house built, they could probably do most of it."

His lips pressed together.

"My uncle owns a construction company in Illinois. You know the unions are so much stronger out there, so my brothers all moved back to work for him." He looked either confused or irritated, maybe both. I stuffed more bread in my mouth.

"And what do you do?" he asked.

Mouth dry and full of half-masticated goo, I reached for the water before I answered. "I'm a financial advisor."

"So, you handle people's money and retirement and stuff?" he asked.

On firmer ground, my voice strengthened. "Yes, I can take care of everything from insurance to old 401Ks to investments."

"Oh, you should have her help you, Max." Becca leaned over to wrap an arm around me. "It's amazing what she can do with money." She leaned her head to speak more softly. "Max lost his grandfather, but he has an inheritance he could use help with."

He looked at Becca as if she'd grown horns.

I sighed at her insensitive mention of Max's loss and reached a hand out to put over his. "I'm so sorry for your loss. No matter how long we have them, losing someone is never easy."

He nodded but pulled his hand away from mine.

Guess I was the only one who felt those sparks.

CHAPTER 3

MAX

M𝚈 ᴇᴀʀꜱ ʙᴜʀɴᴇᴅ, ᴀɴᴅ I ᴅᴏᴡɴᴇᴅ ᴀɴᴏᴛʜᴇʀ ꜰᴇᴡ ɢᴜʟᴘꜱ ᴏꜰ ᴛʜᴇ expensive lager while I eyed the exit. We hadn't even ordered yet, and I didn't know how much longer I could stand this meal. The logical part of my brain yelled for me to sit there and play the nice guy, while the more emotional part begged to make a clean exit. Despite the fact that she seemed sweet and was obviously attractive, I wasn't into one-night stands and if our morals didn't match up, anything more was a no-go.

I adjusted the watch on my wrist and checked the time. Half an hour? It seemed like years.

Feeling everyone's gazes on me, I realized they were waiting for me to say something in response to Cassi's condolences. "Yeah, thank you. He was a hero." I swallowed emotion. "Saved hundreds of lives before he retired."

"Was he a firefighter as well?" Cassi asked.

She seemed so genuine. If I hadn't seen her trying to palm the spoon and tiny gold fork, I wouldn't have believed Becca's stories about her. She'd made it sound like Cassi stole everything she could fit in her purse, and not for any need. Her family was old money.

"Yeah, I'm third generation. I tried to buck the trend after I lost my dad, but I guess it's in the genes."

"You didn't want to be a fireman?" she asked.

Brad jumped in. "In college, Max was convinced he wanted to be a doctor, so he majored in biology." He wiggled his eyebrows suggestively. "Wasn't your favorite class Anatomy and Physiology?" He leaned in to get closer to Cassi. "He can name all your little bits and pieces, and from what I hear through the walls, he knows how to use them."

Becca swatted him in the chest. "Stop trying to embarrass her or you won't be seeing any of my bits and pieces."

Cassi bit her lip and glanced to her lap, unable to meet my gaze. Even if I didn't exactly like her, I didn't want to make her uncomfortable. Pops raised me better than that. I shot Brad a glare. It was an old and very-over-used joke. "Yeah, let me tell you how useless a biology degree is in the real world," I said lightly to move off the subject that obviously mortified Cassi. "I might make fifteen bucks an hour as a lab tech."

"What happened to medical school?" Cassi lifted her head and focused on me, ignoring Brad.

I grimaced. "Turned out it cost too much. My Pops convinced me not to weigh myself down with all that debt."

"He sounds like a smart man." Cassi smiled until tiny lines appeared around her eyes. "If you ever have issues, I'd be happy to help you with any money questions."

"No, thanks," I said more forcefully than I meant to.

Brad sent me a what-the-fuck look, which I shot right back. It was one thing to make me sit through dinner with this chick, but to suggest I trust her with my money? Becca's story about finding an entire drawer full of stolen jewelry, some of it hers, flashed through my mind. All I needed was some advisor to be skimming off the top of my accounts or investing in made-up companies until I had nothing left.

"What I mean is," I said more softly. "It wasn't enough money to be worth your time." I straightened my cramped shoulder muscles and felt a stitch or two pop on my shirt. Shit. I resumed my hunched position. "I'm no millionaire."

Cassi nodded. "Actually, you don't have to be a millionaire. You're the exact type of person I love to work with."

"I bet I am," I huffed under my breath. You think I'm stupid enough not to catch on to you.

"Excuse me?" Cassi's face crumpled, but her voice could have cut glass. "Some advisors want to only work with the rich, but that's not my business model."

I downed the last of my second beer. "Are you sure finances is really the best idea?" I cocked my head to the side. "I mean, considering your past?"

Blue eyes blazed in my direction, just like the hottest part of any fire.

"Are we ready to order?" The waiter saved me from three gawking faces at the table.

"Yup," I answered, picked up the menu for the first time, and closed it again. "Give me whatever is the most expensive dish on the menu."

"That would be our special: fresh Maine lobster, pan seared sea scallops and King crab legs."

God, I hate fish. "Perfect."

CHAPTER 4

CASSI

I FORCED MYSELF TO FOCUS ON BECCA'S OVERLY ANIMATED description of her dress while I scrambled to think of how I'd offended Max. Every word we'd said since he walked in ran through my mind. My heart stopped beating as my blood turned to sludge in my veins—he said he'd heard a lot about me.

My gaze darted to Becca's face. She wouldn't have.

God, if she'd told him the story. Heat rushed to my cheeks, and I wanted to melt in a puddle under the table. It had taken me two years, graduating, and leaving the state for four years, to live that story down. But it would certainly explain his less-than-eager behavior on this date.

I'm going to kill her. I sipped the chocolate martini and let the liquid roll over my tongue before I swallowed. It was amazing.

"I was thinking red, you know, for the holidays. Don't you think?" Becca's gaze rested on me.

Questions begged to jump off my tongue, and I had to bite them back before I demanded to know if Becca had shared my worst secret. She wouldn't have. Would she? I struggled to think of what she'd been saying—bridesmaid dresses. You have at least a year to plan this wedding. "You do whatever you like. Who cares what anyone else thinks?" You never do, anyway. My gaze darted to Max, staring anywhere but at me and nursing his beer. Embarrassment warred with irritation. Irritation won. But I couldn't stand the thought of causing a scene in public. Just the thought of a crowd of people staring at me turned my insides to liquid. I adjusted my attitude to get through the night and said what Becca wanted to hear. "You have impeccable taste. Just look what a great guy Brad is."

Two waiters arrived with the food and set plates in front of us. I picked up the smaller of the forks and stabbed a piece of romaine from my salad. We all busied ourselves with eating. Well, everyone except Max, who took one look at his mouthwatering platter of seafood, nudged it farther away and reached for a roll. I focused on my own food and popped a spicy shrimp into my mouth.

"Actually, it's really important to me what you think." Becca grinned and set her fork down. "We have something to ask you both." She looked up into Brad's face. "You ask, sweetie."

Brad's lips turned up into a smirk. "We didn't just ask you here to get dinner."

A sigh escaped my lips. Thank God, since this blind date is a total shit-show.

"You guys will probably get to know each other pretty well," Brad continued. "If you both say yes to being the best man and the maid of honor."

My gaze darted to Max. He looked like he'd just been asked to make out with a warthog. Spiked sea urchins rolled around my stomach, but I forced a smile to my lips. "Of course. I'd love to be the maid of honor!" If I don't kill the best man and possibly the bride before the wedding.

CHAPTER 5

MAX

THEY MIGHT AS WELL HAVE PUNCHED ME IN THE GUT. I BLINKED and took a drink of water to cover my irritation. I'd known the question was coming, but to put me with Cassi? Who in their right mind would ask her to be the maid of honor? I'd thought Becca had a best friend she was going to ask. Maybe she'd said no?

The smell of the fish was suddenly too much, and I pushed my plate farther away. It didn't help.

"Don't leave me hanging, man," Brad said when I didn't respond.

I opened my mouth, then closed it again, my left hand reaching for my wrist out of habit. The feel of the cool metal watch stopped my snide remark. This wasn't about me. It was about Brad and Becca's wedding. "Of course. Like it was even a question."

"And," Becca said from where she'd snuggled into the crook of Brad's arm, "we've decided to have a combined bachelor and bachelorette party." Her voice was a little loud, the martinis obviously catching up with her. "I know you two won't let me down."

"Looks like we'll be working together a bit." Cassi shot me a wide-eyed look.

I sipped my beer and kept my voice level. "So, you've picked a date for the wedding?"

Becca nodded. "Christmas Eve."

"As in three weeks from now?" I asked.

"It's so perfect," Becca gushed. "The church will be all decorated. I mean, we have to have an afternoon wedding obviously to avoid the evening services, but that's fine. Plus, they had a cancellation at The Drake, so the cost of the reception space will be half of what it would have been—it's good to have friends in the industry."

"They probably had a cancellation because most people have plans for Christmas Eve," Cassi put in a not-so-subtle hint.

"Let me get this straight," I said, not able to fully comprehend the words coming out of her mouth. Brad and I just had a conversation last week about him wanting a long engagement. "You want to get married the day before Christmas? This Christmas?"

"I've always wanted a holiday wedding." Becca smiled up at Brad. "And this is just too perfect to pass up. We're so excited. Aren't we, honey?"

"Of course, sweetie," Brad said, the dutiful fiancé. "Can't wait to have you as my bride."

"You are the best thing that has ever happened to me." She kissed his cheek. "I don't know how I got so lucky to find you."

Brad's cheeks warmed under the praise.

My brain spun. We had a lease. Was Becca moving in? If so, I was moving out.

"Well, this is just so exciting," Cassi said, breaking into my thoughts.

Becca waved between Cassi and me. "Obviously, you two need to exchange numbers so you can get together to plan."

Brad sent me a smile-frosted glare, and I pulled my cell phone from my pocket. "Uh, what's your number, Cassi?"

She rattled off a number with a New York area code and I punched it in my phone and saved it under Klepto, then sent her a text.

"All set," I said and twisted to put the phone in my back pocket. The fabric of my shirt gave up after a valiant effort of holding on. The seam at the top of my shoulder split open. "Oh, damn." I glanced down to see the sleeve drooping and a good portion of my arm exposed.

"Let me help you," Cassi gasped and turned toward me.

"It's fine—" I started.

Her elbow knocked into my nearly full beer, sending the not-so-heavenly lager splashing over my chest and lap. The cold liquid over half my body shocked me to silence, and I held my arms out. Beer dripped from my chin and splashed onto my soaked shirt.

I looked down at the mess of my one fit-for-public outfit. The fabric adhered to my skin and sure enough, the white shirt was now see-through. I scrunched my lips and wiped my hands on a dry section of the tablecloth before I met Cassi's horrified gaze. She looked like she might pass out.

"I'm so sorry," she gasped, and reached over with her napkin to dab at my chest.

I waved her off, the ripped sleeve flapping with my movement. "It's not a problem. It was an old shirt." The shirt really was the last thing I cared about. I didn't want her upset over nothing. Grabbing the fabric, I yanked, and the entire sleeve slid from my arm. "I think I bought it for graduation."

"Damn," Brad coughed to cover a laugh. "Going for the wet T-shirt to impress. Save something for the second date, dude."

Sometimes I really questioned my taste in friends. He really wasn't the same guy around Becca. I dropped the useless sleeve on the table. "I think I'm good for the night." I stood and the manners my grandmother had pounded into my brain from the time I could walk took over. "Cassi, please excuse me. I have to apologize for this mess of an evening, and I think it's time for me to head home."

The horrified expression had solidified on Cassi's features. "I'm so sorry."

"Don't worry about it at all," I said. "I needed a new shirt, anyway."

"You can't leave," Becca announced in a pouty voice that grated on my already frayed nerves. "I'm sure they can find a shirt for you." She leaned into Brad and sent him puppy dog eyes. "This was supposed to be a celebration."

"Come on, Max," Brad said. "Don't let me down."

I took a step away from the table before he could lay the guilt trip on any thicker. "Have a good night." I strode away from the table, ignoring the gaping stares coming from the surrounding tables. Next time they try to goad me into going out, the answer is definitely no.

CHAPTER 6

CASSI

I SETTLED INTO MY NEW OFFICE CHAIR. THE CUSHION EMBRACED my body and some of the tension finally left my shoulders. Friday night left me with a collage of emotions. Everything from anger to anticipation to embarrassment. Mostly embarrassment.

I'd come close at least a hundred times to asking Becca if she'd told Max about my college escapade but never quite got the words out. She'd always loved to make me sound like a complete slut when she told the story.

That has to be what made him act so weird. Before I'd spilled a beer on him. Mortification heated my cheeks once again at the thought of Max, frozen in shock, covered in lager. I shuffled papers and pushed away the image of his shirt shrink-wrapped to his chest—his completely toned and drool-worthy chest. Not to mention his bicep after he ripped the sleeve off.

"All settled in?" My boss's voice broke me from thoughts of which month Max should be on a firefighter calendar.

Papers flew from my hand as I flinched. I cleared my throat and pasted a smile across my face. "Yep." I gathered the papers into a neat stack. "Just getting my organizational system set up."

He raised his eyebrows, obviously not the humorous type. "You sure you don't need anything?"

"I think I've got everything under control." I managed a more even tone. "I've got my call list all set to introduce myself to my new clients, but I'll let you know if I run into any bumps with the system."

"Great," he said. "I'll introduce you to the team at the weekly meeting this Thursday. Becca mentioned that you headed the training team in New York. I was thinking of putting you in a similar position, once you're up to speed on the system, of course."

No pressure at all. Becca had made the introductions that got me this job. Her law firm handled some business for the company, plus her father was friends with the owner. "I did lead the training team. I don't think it should take me long to get the hang of things around here."

"Great, our last lead left a few months ago and since then, the position has been empty." He eyed the mess on my desk. "See you at the meeting on Thursday."

"Looking forward to it." I held the cheerful expression until he disappeared around the corner, then let my head fall to my hands. Great way to make an impression on your first day. Maybe tomorrow I can spill hot coffee on his shirt.

I refocused on writing out my introduction to the clients I'd be taking over. Transitioning to a new financial advisor made most people nervous, so I wanted to come across as competent and knowledgeable. The exact opposite of what I felt right now. Becca had texted five times this morning alone to see if I'd started planning her party, but I ignored her. Work came first.

Getting back to numbers pulled my brain to a more comfortable space. Away from Max. The morning flew by and after my tenth successful call to a new client, I let out a deep breath. Everything's going to be okay.

My phone chimed, and I flipped it over expecting another text from Becca. Instead, my stomach did a weird flip-floppy thing and traded places with my kidney. Max.

"Sorry I didn't get in touch sooner. Brad told me they want to have the bachelor party next weekend, so I guess we need to get on planning."

My shoe tapped out a manic rhythm under my desk. Of course, Becca would be on Brad as well to make sure things were going according to her plans.

"Sure! That sounds great!!" I erased the text and tried for something that didn't sound like a thirteen-year-old wrote it. My fingers hovered over the screen.

"I am available on Saturday or Sunday if that would be convenient for you." Now I'm an uptight prig. Again, I erased the text.

"Sounds like we do need to get some plans going. Would Friday work for you?" I read the text three times, then hit send. As soon as the message zoomed into cyberspace, I wondered if I should have led with another apology for his shirt.

His response came back almost immediately. "I'm on shift Friday through 8am Saturday, sorry. We could meet for dinner Saturday."

"Sure, just let me know a place and time!" I debated on the exclamation point for way too long. Then hit send.

"How about 6 at the Italian deli off Littleton Blvd?"

"See you then." I set my phone down and slumped in my chair like I'd just run a marathon. If every interaction was this taxing, I'd be a pile of mush well before the wedding. At least now I could get Becca off my back about the planning. I didn't remember her being quite so overbearing in college, but it was probably just the stress of the wedding.

I forced my attention back to my list of clients and dialed the next number.

THE WEEK FLEW BY, AND I DID MY BEST TO SETTLE INTO MY NEW job. This offer had been too good to turn down and a part of me knew I'd never be able to move past my last relationship if I stayed in New York. And I really needed to move on.

I threw dress after dress over my shoulder from the boxes stacked in my bedroom. Too formal, too revealing—especially if he'd heard of my escapade—what in the world did someone wear to a not-really-a-date at a deli? Finally, I settled on jeans and a cute blouse with a leather jacket. Winter had settled in over the Rockies and snow was a possibility. At least maybe we'd have a white Christmas.

Not knowing that I was moving back home, my parents had planned a Christmas cruise for themselves. With no other family still in Colorado, and now a wedding on Christmas Eve, it looked like I'd be camping out alone in my barely furnished apartment. The thought didn't inspire any holiday cheer. I'll get a tree and bake some cookies. Alone time will do me good.

I got to the deli fifteen minutes early. It was obviously a family-owned place. The smell of pasta sauce and pizza combined with freshly sliced meats greeted me as I walked through the door. My mouth watered at the savory promise of heaven. Posters of Marilyn Monroe covered every surface of the walls. There was even a life-sized cutout of her in a corner. Someone had put a red scarf and a Santa hat on the cutout to get Marilyn in the holiday spirit.

I grinned and scanned the red booths. My gaze settled on Max's broad shoulders. When he spotted me, he stood, and I fought to keep my relaxed expression in place. He wore a black T-shirt with his firehouse logo across the front and a pair of faded jeans. He looked much more at ease than he had in the slacks and button-up shirt. And way more enticing.

"You found it," he said and stuffed his hands into the pockets of his jeans.

I noticed the same antique watch on his wrist. "Yep, hope you're not too tired after working a long shift."

He shrugged. "I got a nap in. And you get used to it after a while. Let's get some food."

"You'll have to tell me what's good." I followed him to the counter.

"Everything's great, but my favorites are the Mobster or the Godfather."

The guy at the counter obviously knew Max and sent a warm smile my way. "What are you in the mood for today, Max?"

"Hey, Nate. This is Cassi." He waved my way. "I'll do the Godfather, with my usual additions," Max answered and turned to me.

I stared at the handwritten menu of decadent sandwiches, all with their own memorable names. "Well then, I'll try the Mobster."

We picked a booth and sat in awkward silence for a minute while we waited for our food. I wanted to ask him exactly what Becca had told him about me. But how could I explain myself if she had revealed the worst? He'd formed his impression of me and there was nothing I could do about it.

I pulled out my planner and laptop from my bag. "So, I'm thinking Becca is going to want this to be pretty extravagant." I caught his eye roll along with a muffled grunt.

"I was going to suggest we go with the classic strip club," he said.

I snorted. "Much as I would love, and I do mean love, to see her expression, I'd never live that down. Plus, she helped me get this job, so I kind of owe her."

"What? Did she help get some charges off your rap sheet?" Max asked.

I laughed, but then stopped. Wait. Was he serious? He almost sounded serious.

"Here you go." The sandwiches arrived. "One Mobster and one Godfather, double the meat and pepperoncini."

"You are the best, Nate." Max rubbed his hands together and leaned over his sandwich. The colossal structure had to be over six inches tall.

I set my computer aside. Max moaned as he chewed his first bite. I watched while he devoured several more with utter abandon. He was such a different guy from who I'd met at the expensive seafood restaurant. He was so much more relaxed. This was obviously more his element.

"You haven't tried yours," he said, breaking me from my thoughts. "Sorry, I should have picked a different place."

I scrunched my brow and picked up my sub. "Are you kidding? This is perfect. I was just waiting to see if you had a detachable jaw like a snake to actually eat that thing." I took a bite of my own and my eyes went wide. "Wow," I managed after I swallowed. "This is amazing."

The lines on his forehead relaxed. "I thought maybe you like the fancy dining experience."

I shook my head and swallowed another bite. "I had enough high-class, which is code for overpriced, restaurants in New York. They put a tablespoon of whipped potatoes and a sprig of asparagus on your plate with a single shrimp, and you pay fifty bucks." I crunched a potato chip. "This is way more up my alley."

A dollop of mustard sat at the corner of his mouth. He nodded, and a genuine smile spread across his face. A dimple appeared on his right cheek. I'd thought he was handsome before, but that smile sent tingles to some very interesting and forgotten parts of my anatomy.

I cleared my throat and restrained myself from reaching across the table and helping him with the mustard. "How about a party bus?" I blurted. "For the party, I mean. Then we can go to a bunch of different bars and not be stuck in one place."

Over the next hour and a half, we finished the sandwiches,

each using multiple napkins to clean up, and got the rough plans in place for the party. With the expenses resting on us, I tried to keep things reasonable. Talking with Max was actually easy—enjoyable, if I was being honest with myself. He even cracked a joke and gave me another real smile with his dimple coming out to play. Warm, gushy feelings rolled around my chest. "I'll get some calls in for the party bus."

"I'll take care of the guys Brad wants to invite. Can you get in touch with Becca's friends?" Max asked.

"Only if I can have your pickle," I said. His wide eyes darted to my face, and I realized what I'd said. "I mean, I just love pickles. Especially these ones because they're big and spicy. And juicy." My God, stop talking right now. Refusing to give into the embarrassment that wanted to crush me into the floor, I reached across and plucked the untouched garnish from his plate. "What?"

He blinked and shook his head. "Feel free."

"Well, you weren't eating it." I took a bite and forced myself to keep my gaze level while inside I wanted to die.

He cleared his throat, his cheeks tinting red. "So," he said, obviously trying to get the conversation on safer ground. "Do you have family in Denver?"

I nodded and swallowed. "My parents. My brothers all moved out of state."

"Hopefully you didn't have any Christmas Eve plans." He pursed his lips.

I rolled my eyes. "I love Becca, and Brad seems like a great guy, but I have to say it is kind of presumptuous to have a last-minute wedding on Christmas Eve."

"So, you did have plans?" he asked.

"No, my parents didn't know I was moving back," I said. "They'd already paid for a trip over the holidays, so it'll just be me. I'd thought about flying out to visit my brothers in Illinois but with the wedding…" I waved a hand and tried to keep the disappointment from my voice. "It's better. I have a ton of work to do."

Max nodded. "I get the being alone thing. This is the first year I won't have Gram and Pop." He looked away and his voice dropped. "Won't feel like Christmas without her molasses cookies. No one can bake like she could."

My heart squeezed at the obvious pain in his voice. "They raised you?"

"My mom died having me, and my dad died when I was two. So, it was just the three of us."

"He died in a fire?" I asked, then wished I could suck the question out of the air.

"Yeah, he saved a mom, and her two kids, then went back in." He paused. "He didn't make it out."

"Max, I'm so sorry. It sounds like your grandparents were wonderful people." I wanted to reach across the table and take his hand, comfort him, but I remembered how he'd pulled away the other night. "Do you have her recipes?"

His brows pulled together.

"I just meant, if you have her recipes, maybe you can make a batch of the cookies to share with someone special that you're spending the holidays with." I shook my head. "Sorry, that may be too soon. Maybe someday in the future you can use them." Once again, stop talking. "Sorry. I'm going to shut up now."

"No, don't apologize. It's a nice idea." A sad smile creased his face, and he blinked, then straightened. "If I didn't burn the kitchen down. I can cook. We take turns at the station house. But baking isn't my strong suit."

"It would be an adventure." I let my head fall to the side.

"You must have had fun Christmases as a kid with three older brothers."

"Let me tell you, it was loud and there were lots of snowball fights." I laughed as so many memories flooded my mind. "I'm the youngest, so I was always trying to keep up, and there were lots of dart guns involved."

"Sounds like a great time," Max said. "Maybe you should fly out on Christmas day."

I shrugged. "I'll go out for Christmas next year."

He nodded, then grabbed his jacket. "It's getting late, and I have another twenty-four-hour shift tomorrow. But this was fun."

I couldn't miss the surprise in his voice. Hopefully, he'd forgotten I was talking about spicy pickles since he probably already thought I was a hussy. I dropped the unfinished half on my plate and packed up my notes and computer.

"I'll meet you outside." Max dropped a tip on the table and walked toward to the restroom.

As soon as he rounded the corner, I dropped my head to the table. Pickles? I mean, I did love pickles, and it was a travesty to let them go to waste. But seriously? Spicy pickles. He must think I'm a total freak.

I lifted my head, then stood by the booth. The crumpled bills took my focus away from the pickle incident. Small family-owned places were nearly impossible to keep going with their slim profit margins. I took out my purse to add to the tip. My OCD with money made me grab Max's bills and organize them along with mine by denomination and facing the same direction.

"What are you doing?" Max practically growled from behind me.

I jumped and dropped my still open purse on the seat of the booth. "I was—"

The fury in his face stopped my words. Not a trace of the sadness or emotions over his grandparents remained.

"They depend on tips to keep this place going." He grabbed the now perfectly organized cash from my hand and slapped it on the table, then put the saltshaker on the bills—a little harder than necessary.

I gaped, but finally found my voice. "I have a thing about organizing money. It comes with being in finance."

"Yeah, sure." He motioned toward the door, his face hard as cement.

Just like that, all the warm sappy feelings were gone, and it was like a wall came down between us. Not just any wall—more like the Great Wall of China, topped with barbed wire and booby traps.

I swallowed and gathered my purse and computer bag. I just can't do anything right with this guy.

CHAPTER 7

MAX

I watched Cassi drive out of the parking lot. To think I'd been having a good time talking to her. I even told her about my parents and Gram's cookies. I'd forgotten for an hour or two that she had a serious problem. To steal silverware from a fancy restaurant was bad enough, but to steal a tip off the table of a small business? That was a special kind of messed up.

I don't care how great her sense of humor is or how much of a knockout she is. That relationship is something that will never happen. Being raised by my grandparents had influenced me a lot. Some might say for the worse—like Becca, who thought opening doors for women was an offense to their feminine power. But one thing they taught me was the difference between right and wrong, and there was no moral gray area here. Cassi wasn't starving or trying to feed her kids. She was just a plain thief.

A sour taste filled my mouth. I'd plan this party and go to the wedding, but then I'd never see this woman again.

I drove home to get some sleep before my shift. Working twenty-four on and twenty-four off could leave you feeling constantly hung over if you didn't take care of yourself. And when I was off my game people could die.

Brad was home watching the Avalanche game when I got back to the apartment. A glitzy fake Christmas tree sat in the corner. The purple bulbs and pink tinsel glowed with the neon white LED lights and cast the room in an almost floral vibe. I held up a hand to block the gaudy mess. "Becca was here, I'm guessing?"

"Yeah, sorry. I know we weren't going to decorate, but she said our place needed some Christmas cheer." He shook his head. "It just made her so happy that I couldn't say no."

I didn't want Christmas cheer. I didn't want Christmas at all. This was the first year I wouldn't have Grams or Pops to be with. If I had my way, we'd skip straight to January. I bit my tongue against the not-so-nice comments begging to be released as I walked over and yanked the plug from the outlet... and I could see again.

"Man, that is so much better. I think my vision is permanently impaired. I'm not sure about those lights." Brad blinked.

I snorted. "Yeah, but the bulbs and tinsel are so much better."

With the wedding on Christmas Eve, Brad would be gone for Christmas day. We'd planned on an all-day movie marathon. Not only would I not have my grandparents, but I'd also be completely alone. I'll trade for a shift. I pushed the sadness away and locked it down tight.

"Anyway, how was your date?" Brad asked.

I tossed my keys into the dish and sat in my favorite chair, a worn leather recliner that had seen better days but was wide enough to fit my shoulders and supported my back perfectly. "It wasn't a date." I leaned back and ignored his raised eyebrows. "You're lucky I'm a good friend."

"Come on," he exclaimed. "I set you up with a hot chick for the wedding and all I get is grief."

"Not happening," I said.

"I'm sorry, man." His tone shifted, obviously hearing my irritation. "Hey, a package came for you." He motioned to a box on the table next to my chair.

I picked up the box and sliced the tape with the utility knife I always carried in my pocket. Inside was a white button-down shirt. I didn't recognize the brand, but it looked expensive. A note was written on the bottom of the shipping slip: Sorry about your shirt. The least I could do was replace it. ~Cassi

I tossed the box aside. Wonder who she ripped off to pay for that.

"I really appreciate you doing all this and especially on such short notice," Brad said.

"Yeah, about that. What happened to a long engagement?" I'd held off asking the question all week, not wanting to stir up trouble, but at some point, the issue of the living situation had to be addressed.

"Well, you know how Becca can get." He sighed and put his hands behind his head, glancing at the Christmas tree. "She was dead set on a holiday wedding, and when this opened up there was no stopping her."

"We just signed another year lease."

"I'm sorry. I should have talked to you." He sounded sincere, but that didn't help pay the rent. He never stood up to this woman.

"So, what's the plan?" He knew I couldn't afford this place on my own and finding a one bedroom in my price range would also be a stretch.

"I'm open to whatever works," he said. "I mean, you're gone for entire days. Becca could move in here with us or I could move to Becca's place, but then you'd need another roommate."

From his tone, I gathered Becca wasn't so open. I raised my eyebrows.

"Becca wants me to move in with her. She has it all furnished and set up the way she likes it. Not so masculine and bachelor pad." He dropped his hands and leaned forward. "I really love her, Max. I want to make her happy."

But does she make you happy? I bit the question back. It wasn't my life. "Sounds like the decision's already been made."

"I'll pay my half of the rent until you find a new roommate," Brad said. "Or if you want to break the lease, I'll pay the fee."

I got up and headed for my room. "No worries, man. I got the money from Pops." Not much, but you don't need to worry about that. "I'll figure it out. Last thing you need when you're starting out is two rents." I closed the door and got ready for bed. I lay in the dark, staring at the ceiling for several minutes. Most likely I'd have to move farther away from the station house to afford rent. But that was a problem for tomorrow. I rolled over and forced my brain to turn off.

Cassi and I kept as much of the party planning to text as possible, but a meeting to go over final details was inevitable. Especially since we needed to see the private room at the club where we planned on ending the night. Some in style place called The Lounge. Renting the room for a few hours was going to cost more than one month of my rent. The things we do for friends.

But Brad had been there for me through some rough times. Losing Grams was bad enough, but having to put Pops in hospice and then losing him had almost broken me. Brad helped pick up the pieces. And I still enjoyed hanging out with him—when Becca wasn't there for him to impress.

I shut off the car and sat in the parking place outside the club. I had to gather my strength to deal with Cassi. It would have been easier if I just couldn't stand her. But I'd had fun with her at the deli the other day. She was down to earth—nothing like the spoiled rich chick Becca had described. However, when I'd walked out of the bathroom and saw her about to pocket the tip, I'd wanted to puke.

I opened the door and headed into the club. This early in the afternoon, only staff were around.

A hostess paused in wiping down menus and approached me. "Can I help you?"

"I'm here to see the private lounge for a bachelor party." I glanced around the glitzy space. The high ceilings had exposed ductwork and pipes, more of the industrial vibe, but the tables and other furnishings were all glitz and glamor. Christmas lights on fake palm trees were supposed to get the place in the holiday spirit. I could see why Cassi suggested the club. Perfect for Becca, and available on short notice. "I'm supposed to be meeting someone, though."

My phone buzzed in my pocket. Cassi. I hit the green button. "Hey."

"Hey." Her voice sounded way too cheerful. "I'm so sorry. I have a bit of an emergency at work and I'm not going to make it."

"Do we need to reschedule?" I asked, as a mixture of relief and something else washed over me.

"No," she said, and what sounded like papers shuffled in the background. "I trust your judgement. If you like it, let's just book it. We're kind of down to the wire and, to be honest, I can't spend more time calling places to find an opening. Between my new job and the bridesmaid duties..."

Being Becca's maid of honor sounds about as fun as getting a lobotomy with a rusty spoon. "I'll text you and let you know."

"Thanks so much, Max." She ended the call.

I slipped my phone back into my pocket and returned my attention to the hostess.

"Would you like me to show you the VIP room?" she asked.

"No." I shook my head. "Go ahead and book it, please."

Her eyebrows shot up. "Are you sure? I'd be happy to take you back."

I waved her off. "You need a credit card?"

Five minutes later, I walked back to my truck and drove out of the parking lot. The space took a thousand-dollar deposit. Plus, I was supposed to buy them a gift for the party and the wedding. This best man crap was a racket.

CHAPTER 8

CASSI

I yanked the tenth dress over my shoulders and gritted my teeth against screaming. With the wedding being so close, we were left with shopping off the rack for the bridesmaid dresses. Not a simple task when Becca insisted on having four brides-maids, plus her maid of honor. This was the second upscale bridal boutique we'd gone to. At least this one had a good stock of red dresses.

"You're sure everything is set for the party?" Becca called over the curtain of the fitting room. "I mean, we need this to be epic."

If you wanted epic, maybe you should have picked a date further out than three weeks and not right before Christmas. "It's going to be great. Max said the VIP space was perfect, and I booked the bus myself."

"Wait, you didn't actually see the VIP room?" Becca asked. I heard the frown in her voice. "I thought you said you were meeting there to check it out."

I closed my eyes and swore. Getting up to speed enough to take over the training team had put a ton of extra work on my plate. Plus, Becca had been taking up way too much of my time with constant calls and texts about the wedding details. If I heard the words *I need my maid of honor* one more time, I'd likely jump off the nearest balcony. "I saw pictures."

"You specifically told me you were going to see it." Her voice rose. "I'm not sure about Max's judgement."

Mercy, our friend from college who'd recently moved back, piped up from her stall where she was trying on a dress. We'd been inseparable freshman and sophomore year—the triplets, we'd called ourselves. But she and I lost touch right after she moved away. "I've been to The Lounge. The VIP room is great. Don't worry, Becca."

"Hmph," Becca snorted. "If it's a sleazy place, Max is going to have to deal with me."

I pulled the curtain open and held out my hands for her opinion on the hideous swath of bright red fabric strangling my body. Mercy stepped out of her stall. The dress at least didn't smash her boobs like pancakes, and she had some room in the hips, whereas I was afraid the fabric would give at any moment.

Max's shirt ripping flashed across my mind, and my cheeks heated to match the dress. I firmed my resolve to ask Becca what she'd told him about me. Today. The man had been popping up in my head way too often. Especially after our conversation at the deli. But he switched from the epitome of a great guy to a world-class ass at a moment's notice.

Mercy's cute little baby bump dragged me away from racy thoughts about Max. She now looked twice the size in the cut of the dress. On her, the only place the dress stretched tight was over her pregnant belly—the reason she needed a larger size—but the fabric hung loose over every other part of her.

I raised my brows and bit my lips to hide a laugh.

She fake-glared and molded her hands around the mound of her tummy. "I know. It makes me look like I'm ten months along."

"It's sweet," I said as my own ovaries squeezed at the thought of a family. I'd always said before I was thirty. Wasn't looking so likely now. "You're a beautiful pregnant mermaid."

A wiggle and a tug adjusted the torture rag so I could at least breathe. I needed one size bigger to fit my curves, but this was all they had close to my size, and Becca's sister, Hannah, needed the only one they had a few sizes larger.

I waddled out like a penguin. The dress squeezed my legs to the knee then flared out in a mermaid style, the satin giving way to an explosion of chiffon. I waited while Becca glanced between Mercy and me. "Hannah," she called to her sister. "Come out. We're all waiting."

"I don't think this one is good." A small voice came from the next dressing room.

"Come out and let me be the judge." Becca crossed her arms. "I'm the bride, after all."

The curtain pulled back, and Hannah waddled out. The fabric barely contained her ample chest. Her expression hurt my heart. She was miserable.

Becca held out her arms. "Oh, look at you guys! So beautiful. I think this is the one."

Mercy and I shared a what-the-hell-she's-gone-nuts look. I cleared my throat. "You really think so? The second one was much simpler, and they had more sizes." I mean, it was terribly ugly, but at least we didn't feel like half covered idiots.

"But these make a statement. I've always loved the drama of the mermaid cut." Becca nodded to herself and walked around her sister, then leaned in but spoke loud enough for everyone to hear. "You'll have to go on a diet, of course."

Hannah shot me a look that screamed help, then her head dropped.

That's it. I penguin walked around the plush open area of the fitting rooms, making an arc around the circular creamy leather settee. "You seriously want us waddling down the aisle?" I threw my hands to the sides. "I don't even have heels on. And we're just guessing about the sizes for the two other bridesmaids. These dresses are so fitted. They might not even be able to zip them."

Becca's mouth pursed, and I wondered when she'd become quite so ridiculously narcissistic. Having had a long-distance friendship for the past four years, I'd never seen this side of her. She was funny and great to talk to and spunky. Plus, she'd talked me through first being with an alcoholic boyfriend, then getting up the nerve to leave him. There were months when we'd talked every day on the phone. Her behavior now had to be because she was stressing about the wedding.

Mercy joined me in a tottering parade. "I'll be taking bets on who faceplants down the aisle. I'm betting on myself." She stumbled as if on cue and jerked upright, holding her belly. "See? That will definitely make a memorable wedding. There goes the pregnant one. Down for the count."

We stopped and waited, hoping bridezilla wasn't about to make an entrance and rip our heads off.

Becca stared and blinked slowly, then let out a bark of a laugh. "Oh my God, you're so right. I mean, you all look beautiful, but that would have ruined everything." She sighed and rubbed her eyes. "I'm just so stressed about this wedding. I had no idea it would be so hard to pull this together."

Relief cooled the irritation threatening to bubble over. "Hey, it's a lot. Most people plan their weddings for a year or more." I grinned. "You just have to be the overachiever and do it in a month."

"Overachiever or moron. The jury's still out." She took a long drink of the sparkling water the boutique supplied. "Plus, my mom is angry they have to cut their trip short to get here for the wedding. I'm second-guessing everything. I didn't mean to take it out on you."

Hannah let out a sigh and mouthed a thank you behind Becca's back. I sent her a wink. Poor kid. Having the ever-perfect Becca as an older sister had to be tough.

I remembered Becca's mom as a perfectionist. Compared to her, Becca looked like a mess. "When are they coming back?"

"Not until the morning of the wedding." Becca sighed.

"Then we don't have to worry about her right now," I said.

"Okay." Becca waved to the attendant who'd been smart enough to hide out of the way. "Let's see the second ones again."

I glanced at my watch. At this rate, I'd be up most of the night getting the financial reports ready for my meetings tomorrow.

An hour later, I waved goodbye to Mercy. "Call me. We need to catch up." She'd switched schools junior year—right after my escapade—to go to San Diego since her dream was to save the dolphins. Turned out she got seriously seasick and was terrified of sharks. That had to be a good story.

"Definitely, I've got a ton going on with Christmas parties and now the wedding and stuff, but for sure after the holidays."

Hannah sent a shy wave and rushed out the door. At least the dresses we'd settled on were the right sizes, although now instead of demonic mermaids we looked more like curtains straight out of the seventies. But they were still flaming red to satisfy Becca and her holiday theme. Really, that color didn't compliment anyone.

I fell in step beside Becca as we left the bridal boutique. The thought of bringing up the mishap in college, even to Becca, made me shaky. With my stomach twisted like a pretzel, I took the plunge. "I have something I've been meaning to ask you."

She tied the belt of her coat against the chilly December air. Her heels clicked along the sidewalk. "How about we grab a bite to eat? I have some more wedding stuff I need your help on."

"Actually, I have a ton of work to get done tonight." I held onto my gumption. "This shouldn't take long."

She stopped in front of her car, the look on her face less than happy.

The words tumbled out. "Did you tell Max about what happened in college?"

"What happened in college?" She wrinkled her nose. "A lot happened in college."

"Becca, come on." A sick feeling crept its way up my throat. "Did you tell him about the dean?"

"Are you still freaking out over that whole thing?" Her brows pulled together. "Cassi, it's ancient history. No big deal."

"No big deal? I woke up naked. In the dean's pool. Floating on a blow-up swan. He found me." My hands gripped my purse like I was going to use it as a weapon. "I caused his divorce."

"Well, it was your idea to go skinny dipping in his pool." She held my gaze and tilted her head slightly to the side.

I didn't remember any of that portion of the night. It was blocked by booze. "They called me the Swan Princess for two years." I couldn't take any more of this. "Just tell me if Max knows."

"I never told Max. But I remember telling Brad. I tell him everything," she said, and a look flitted across her face that I couldn't place. Then it was gone, and confident Becca was back.

Really? Everything? I doubt that. You weren't always this proper lawyer lady.

"I suppose it's possible he told Max. It's a good story. Especially when I tell it." She snickered. She actually laughed.

I nearly swung my purse at her head.

Possibly seeing her imminent death, she sobered and gripped my arms. "I'm sorry. I just figured it's been long enough that you can laugh about it now."

My voice came out quaking. "It was one of the worst experiences of my life."

The smile slipped from her face like snow melting in the Colorado sunshine. "I'm sorry." Her eyes went round. "Oh, my God. Is that why he was acting so weird at dinner?"

"It has to be," I said. "Why else?"

She pulled me into a hug. "I'm really sorry, Cassi. I had no idea you'd ever be moving back and even meet him."

At least I know now. A bit of my anger over how Max had

acted dissolved in the acid of my stomach. He probably thought I was a home wrecking, crazy drunk.

"I'll straighten it all out," Becca said, then released me.

"No," I exclaimed. "Don't say anything. Not to Brad or Max. It's not worth it."

"Are you sure?" Becca's gaze studied my face. "I'm the worst friend."

"No, you're not." I patted her arm and sighed. "Max and I wouldn't have worked out, anyway." Even as I said the words, I couldn't help but wonder what would have happened if he'd never heard the story.

CHAPTER 9

MAX

Snow fell in fluffy clumps outside my window. So peaceful. The exact opposite of the turmoil going on inside me. With every day that passed, Christmas got closer. Everyone else seemed to be getting into the spirit. Tins of cookies and other sweets showed up at the station house by the hour. None of them held a candle to Gram's. The thought was nice, but with every red bow or tree I saw, another grain of sadness weighed me down.

I shook off the heaviness and refocused. Tonight was the big night. The bachelor party. I tucked extra cash in my pocket and clasped Pop's watch on my wrist.

"Hey," Brad called from the hallway. "Are you ready?"

"Yeah," I said and walked out my door.

"Let's get this party started." Brad adjusted his jacket, then eyed me. "You sure you're up for this?"

"Ready to have some fun." I nodded and forced a smile. I'd ended up working five shifts on, five off. More days than they usually scheduled in a row, but a virus had half the department out sick. My body needed rest, and I'd felt hungover all day.

I threw my leather jacket over the shirt Cassi had sent me. Her apology gift was the only thing in my closet appropriate to wear. The one other dress shirt I owned I'd bought for the funerals and that was stuffed in the farthest recesses of my closet. A likely stolen shirt would have to do. At least it fit. I could even raise my arms without fear of tearing the seams.

The bus was downstairs waiting, having already picked up the girls from Becca's apartment and the rest of Brad's friends from farther north. I sucked in a breath of freezing air to brace myself, then climbed aboard. Hoots and screeches greeted our entrance. The bus held forty, and we were pushing that limit.

Becca, decked out in some sparkling minidress, ran over, and threw herself against Brad and grinned at me. "Max, looking dapper in that shirt." She slid a headband over my hair that read Best Man. "Ready for an epic night?"

"Can't wait," I said.

She leaned past me and laid a kiss on Brad. When she pulled back, she smiled up at him. "I'm the luckiest girl in the world, you know that?"

"And that's my cue," I mumbled and slipped past to find a seat. Everyone was hitting the bar pretty hard, from the looks of it. I grabbed a bottle of water and took a swig, then took the headband off and tossed it aside. From across the bus, Cassi sent me a civil wave, wearing her very own Maid of Honor headband. Next to her sat a woman with a Bridesmaid headband and a very pregnant belly.

I returned the wave. This is going to be a long night.

Someone cranked the music up to ear bleeding decibels and we rolled down the street.

We went from dance club to dance club. All the clubs were pretty much the same—too much loud music, too much drinking, and too many people. I spent most of my time checking for fire safety violations just to keep my mind occupied. The one bit of fun I had was bothering the manager until he moved a Christmas tree from blocking a fire exit. He called me a grinch.

By the third stop, I was looking for any excuse I could to get out of the night. We piled on the bus, and I slouched in a corner. Maybe if I just didn't get on at the next stop, no one would notice. I glanced at the emergency exit five feet from where I sat. Or maybe I could jump out the back at the next stoplight.

I watched the twinkling lights of the decorated trees and buildings go by and sank deeper into my dislike of the holiday cheer. Everywhere I looked was red and green and tinsel.

A warm body collapsed next to me. I straightened and turned. Cassi blinked at me with pupils that told me she'd been enjoying the free drinks at the clubs. Her voice was relaxed, but her words weren't slurred. Too much. "We need to talk."

I leaned as far back as my seat and the wall next to me would allow. "Party planning?"

"I'm not a hussy," she proclaimed.

My brows shot through the roof of the bus. "I never said you were." A thief, yes. But I never said anything about being a hussy. "I don't know—"

"No," she interrupted. "You just listen for a minute. I was in college. We all do stupid things in college." She squinted her eyes at me. "Did you never do anything stupid? Mr. I'm-so-perfect with your muscles and your lips and those damn eyes. Wait, now I sound like a hussy."

I held up a hand to stop her.

She sniffed and refocused. "I guess it was my idea to go skinny-dipping in the dean's pool. I just remember waking up floating naked on that damn swan."

Wait, what? My hand fell to my side. I shoved away an image of Cassi naked, floating on a pool swan.

"The dean was worried I'd fall off and drown. He wasn't even supposed to be home." The words flowed like a waterfall. "He was wrapping me in towels and asking if I was okay and then his wife shows up." She waved her hands in the air. Her drink flew from the cup and sloshed over two girls dancing in the aisle.

"Hey!" they exclaimed. One wiped the alcohol from her leg with her Santa hat.

Cassi sent an annoyed glance over her shoulder. "Yeah, sorry." She dropped the empty cup to the floor, and I upped my estimation of how much she'd had to drink. She tried to flip her hair over her shoulder and winced as the strands tangled in the Maid of Honor headband. She ripped the plastic from her head and tossed it after the cup. "Anyway, she gets all screaming about him having an affair with a student and calls the campus police to report him. And I'm there naked, no clothes anywhere to be found. Then the house fills with all these people. I couldn't even tell them how I'd gotten there."

Now I really want to hear the end of this story. I forced my face to stay neutral.

"The investigation was terrible. It lasted months, and I had to tell my story over and over, then testify in front of a panel. My worst moment playing out for everyone to judge. I mean, I never planned on wrecking a marriage." Her eyes filled with tears. "Then everyone called me the Swan Princess for the next two years, and I mean everyone. I'd walk around campus and hear it behind me. People would slip notes in my bag about what a slut I was. But I probably deserved it. I ruined a man's life. She divorced him, and even though I told the truth, she used me against him to get a settlement."

The bus went around a turn, and she swayed in her seat. I reached out to steady her, so she didn't go toppling into the aisle, and she gripped my hand.

"The dean kept his job, but there were always people talking," she continued after the bus straightened out. "And it wasn't like another school would hire him even after the panel found that there was no inappropriate behavior on his part. I had to leave the state after graduation. I mean, I had to get away. Sometimes I'm still freaked out about being in public. Like I'll see someone and think, what if they recognize me?"

I snapped my hanging jaw shut, completely speechless. This girl had a whole host of problems, kleptomania possibly being the least of it. I took my handkerchief from my pocket and handed it to her as a fat tear rolled down her cheek.

She sniffed and patted my arm. "I had to tell you, so you knew my side of the story."

I just nodded.

"You don't think I'm a hussy, do you?" she asked and wiped her tears.

"No, it sounds like you were in the wrong place at the wrong time." I spoke the truth. I felt bad for her. How many college kids do dumb stuff? To get caught was one thing. To have it played out for everyone to see was a whole other matter. It took a lot of nerve for her to stay at the school and not transfer. "I don't think it was your fault at all."

"Really?" She let out an enormous sigh.

The bus stopped at The Lounge, much to my relief. This was the final club and people started filing off. I grabbed a water bottle and pressed it into Cassi's hand. "You'll thank me tomorrow."

She nodded. "Yeah, I think I've had enough to drink. I was trying to work up the nerve to talk to you."

I paused. Why was it so important to her that she tell me that story? If it had happened to me, I'd bury that crap and never bring it up. We paraded into the club. Music blared so loud the bass drummed in my lungs. I glanced over the packed dance floor, then, out of habit, my gaze found the two fire exits. No Christmas trees blocking these ones.

Cassi slipped into a booth in the VIP area, which was a little quieter than the main room, waving off calls from the other girls to come to the dance floor. I took a seat beside her. At least in here people could talk. With her confessing mood, I almost wanted to ask her about the stealing—if she'd ever gotten help and if it was still a problem, especially given her profession.

"You wore it," she said when I took off my jacket.

"What?" I asked.

She motioned to my torso, and I looked down at the shirt. "Oh, yeah. Thanks. You didn't need to do that."

"It looks really nice on you." She sounded sincere.

A cocktail waitress approached, and we ordered waters.

Over an hour and three waters later, another waitress decked out as a sexy elf came to the table. This one carried a long pole with a string attached. As she dangled the string over our heads, I saw the mistletoe tied to the end.

"You two are under the mistletoe," she shouted loud enough for everyone to hear over the music. Everyone in the party stopped their conversations and turned to look.

"It's tradition that you kiss," the elf announced.

I swallowed past a dry throat and darted a glance at Cassi, who was about the shade of a poinsettia.

"Kiss, kiss, kiss," everyone in the VIP room chanted.

"What do you think?" I asked. Tradition be damned. I wasn't about to kiss her if she didn't want me to. Even if every time she smiled, which wasn't often around me, the thought crossed my mind.

"Well," she smiled shyly. "I think it's bad luck if we don't."

I leaned forward, but paused and met her gaze. She nodded. I lowered my lips to hers. Soft and warm and sweet.

Something stirred deep in my chest, like an ember being stoked and brought to life. Instead of the peck I'd been planning on, the kiss turned into something else. Longer and deeper.

Hoots and whistles broke me from the haze, and I pulled away. Cassi met my gaze with surprise that mirrored my own. The cheering died down and the kissing elf moved on to another table.

Brad sat in the seat across from us. His gaze darted between us. "Am I interrupting anything?"

Cassi straightened and shifted away from me.

"No." I moved to give her some distance and tried to ignore the weird feeling in my chest. "Not at all. What's up, man?"

"I just wanted to thank you two for putting this together." He waved to where Becca was dancing, the center of attention where she liked to be. "She's thrilled."

"Not a problem," I said, and slipped my hand over my wrist to adjust my watch. But all my fingers touched was skin, no metal. My gaze snapped to my wrist. The watch was gone. My grandfather's watch.

Already frazzled neurons, tired after too many shifts in a row, then completely thrown off by the kiss on top of Cassi's confession, sputtered and snapped. My hand shook as I lifted my naked wrist, the skin neon white where the watch should have been. "It —it's gone"

Cassi's brow furrowed. "What are you talking about?"

I couldn't rip my gaze away from my bare wrist. The watch had been a tenth anniversary present for Pops from Gram. She'd saved for two years to buy it for him. It was his most prized possession, especially after we lost Gram.

"Oh shit," Brad exclaimed. "Your watch. When was the last time you had it?"

"Here," I said, going over it in my head. "Five minutes ago."

Ripping the napkin out of my lap, I leapt from the booth, praying the watch would be on the seat. Nothing. No, it's not possible. It can't be gone. I fell to the floor and leaned under the booth to search.

"Don't worry. We'll find it," Brad said. "I'm sure it has to be here."

Then it hit me. She'd taken it. The rich, kleptomaniac who could buy herself anything but got off on stealing other people's prized possessions. The embers in my chest burst into flames and burned away the warm, fuzzy emotions of minutes before. This was enough. I didn't care about some stupid kiss—hell, that was probably when she grabbed it.

I hadn't called her out on the silverware or the tip at the deli, but she wasn't getting away with this. Disgust permeated my voice. I got to my feet and stared straight at Cassi. "Did you tell me that sob story so I'd let my guard down? I'm not some idiot you can distract with a kiss and rip off. Give. It. Back."

CHAPTER 10

CASSI

My eyes widened as I took in the extremely pissed-off guy who only a few minutes before I'd been kissing.

"You think I have your watch?" I gasped.

"I'll say this one more time. Give it back before I call the police and have your crazy ass thrown in jail."

His voice left no room for doubt. He'd gone insane. Snapped.

"I don't have it." My voice came out shaking, but not from fear or the alcohol leaving my system. Rage at his accusation left me trembling with fury. My integrity was something I valued most. I'd never steal a penny, much less someone's family heirloom.

Brad stood and put a hand on Max's chest. "Dude, calm down, and we'll figure this out. I'm sure Cassi has nothing to do with the watch."

Max turned his daggers on Brad. "How can you say that when you know what she is?"

My jaw clenched. What exactly am I?

"Is there a problem?" the waitress asked, her forehead wrinkled in concern as other tables and some of the dancers took notice of our display.

"No, no problem," Brad tried to laugh it off. "Just a misunderstanding."

"Yes, there is a problem," Max shouted and pointed a finger at me. "She stole my watch."

The gazes of the entire party weighed on me like a thousand bricks, but I refused to duck my head. Instead, I sat straighter and lifted my chin. The music that had seemed so loud before now couldn't be loud enough to cover my embarrassment. I met Mercy's wide-eyed gaze.

Becca jogged up from the dance floor, her face flushed with alcohol and exertion. Two bouncers followed her, obviously noticing the strife.

The waitress glanced between me and Max. "You lost your watch, sir?"

"No, I didn't lose it. She stole it." He mumbled something under his breath, but all I caught were the swear words.

"That's ridiculous," Becca jumped in to defend me. "The clasp needed to be fixed when you got it. You can't possibly think Cassi would steal it."

Max stared at her as if he'd never seen her before and shook his head.

"Let me check the booth for you, sir," the waitress said. "You'd be amazed at what we find between the cushions." She bent and ran her hand in the crook of the seat.

Max waved his hand at me. "You've been telling me stories for the last year about your kleptomaniac roommate who steals everything. And now you expect me to believe it is just a coincidence that a very expensive antique watch disappeared?" His face flushed and veins popped out on his neck. "How could you even set me up with her?" He turned to Becca, whose mouth was open, but she never got a chance to get a word out. "And why the hell would you want her as your maid of honor? She'll probably steal all the wedding cash!"

I closed my eyes as pieces fell into place. God, this was why he's been acting so weird. It had nothing to do with the dean and the investigation.

A hand popped up beside me. "Is this it?" the waitress asked. "It was pretty far back there, but I don't think it's damaged."

The watch dangled from her fingertips.

Max's mouth closed and opened repeatedly in a gape-mouth-fish-impersonation.

"You thought I was Caroline?" I wasn't sure if I should be relieved or angry. "Why?"

Max's stare bounced between our three faces as Becca's mouth dropped.

"Oh, that explains so much!" Becca gasped. "See, it had nothing to do with your being the Swan Princess."

I flinched at her use of the horrible nickname.

"But," Max managed. "You tried to steal the spoon and the gold fork at the restaurant."

Brad took the watch and apologized to the waitress. "Dude, they had four roommates in college. Cassi is Becca's best friend." He pressed the watch into Max's hand. The clasp dangled, broken. "Caroline is the one you heard those stories about."

"I knocked the spoon off the table. Because you made me nervous. I hadn't been on a date in over a year." Anger was winning. Anger at Max for thinking I could steal his watch. Anger at Becca for calling me the Swan Princess. But mostly anger at myself for enjoying when he kissed me.

"Now that that's all out of the way, we can get back to party-ing!" Becca exclaimed. "No need to bring up the past."

I slanted a glare her way.

Max looked between me and the watch. "You weren't going to steal the tip at the deli?" He ran a hand over his face and glanced toward the ceiling. He looked horrified. "I'm such an idiot." With a deep breath, he straightened his shoulders and turned to me. "I'm so sorry. I have no idea what to even say besides I'm so sorry. I was rude."

"Yes, you were." I crossed my arms. This was all too much. Everyone staring at me brought back memories of walking across campus while people pointed and laughed behind their hands. I wasn't like Becca. I didn't like being the center of attention. Maybe that was why we'd been friends. She soaked up the attention that I didn't want. But in this huge space, feelings of claustrophobia smothered me.

"Come on. This is my bachelorette party." Becca tugged on my arm. "Let's just have fun."

I shook my head. "I've had enough fun. I'm leaving."

"You don't have a ride," Max said. "We came in the bus."

I was already walking out of the VIP room. "I can figure it out. Don't worry, I'm not going to steal a car."

I STAYED IN BED HALF OF THE NEXT DAY, UNABLE TO FACE THE reality of the mess that was my life. Mercy texted me and I told her I was fine. She asked to meet for lunch, but I begged off. There was a lot to do before the wedding and I had a ton of work to get done for my new clients.

A knock at my door jerked me from where I was lying on the couch typing out a proposal for a retirement overhaul. "Who is it?"

"It's your best friend who you've been ignoring all day," Becca called through the door.

I chewed on the inside of my lip while I wondered if I could handle seeing her at the moment. The sound of her voice calling me the Swan Princess rang in my ears.

"Cassi, I'm so sorry that I ever introduced you to that shmuck. I can't believe the things he was saying about you after you left," she called through the door.

Oh, hell no. I yanked the door open. "What did he say?"

She adapted her typical oh-my-God-you're-not-going-to

believe-this look and brushed past me. "He was trying to say you not only threw yourself at him, you practically begged him. Then he said you were badmouthing me and Brad, saying I was a terrible friend and what a lowlife Brad is."

I stared, too shocked to get words out past my frozen tongue.

She scrunched her lips and nodded. "Oh, trust me. I gave him a piece of my mind. I wasn't about to believe that you called me names like that."

"Names like what?" I managed. "I never said anything." Did I? I was complaining about how demanding Becca was being.

"Bridezilla, controlling bitch, narcissistic," she said. "Stuff like that."

"Those words have never left my mouth." Though I thought a couple of them. "And he's got some nerve to say I threw myself at him." The kiss and the heat I'd felt with his lips on mine flashed through my brain. To think I'd let him kiss me.

"He was trying to save face after the scene he made. I didn't believe him, and neither did Brad. It was probably the alcohol talking." She sat on the couch, my lone piece of furniture in the living room.

I frowned. "Did he start drinking after I left?"

"What?"

"He was drinking water all night." I searched her expression.

She tilted her head to the side. She didn't blink, didn't hesitate. "A few shots, in short order, can do a number on people. You know that."

I nodded, but her words didn't settle right. I pushed the feeling away. "I guess he was upset after the whole watch thing."

She shrugged. "Anyway, Brad straightened him out and you'll never have to talk to him again."

"He's not going to be at the wedding?" Tight muscles in my neck relaxed at the thought.

"Well, he'll be there, but you don't have to talk to him and then you never have to see him again." She waved a hand.

My muscles snapped back taut. I closed my eyes against the nausea that erupted at the thought of being in the same room as Max.

"Speaking of calling people names," she said. "I shouldn't have used that terrible nickname."

I swallowed past a surprisingly thick throat and lied. "It's okay."

"No, it isn't." She stood up. "You're my best friend and I was drunk, but that's no excuse. Especially after everything you've put up with from me over the past few weeks."

"I forgive you." I pulled her in for a hug. Staying mad at Becca took a ton of energy that I didn't have. I needed my best friend. "Let's not mention birds of any type again, deal?"

"Deal." She stepped away. "Now, we really need to work on getting you some furniture and decorating."

I sighed. "This is a month-to-month lease. I haven't found a permanent place yet."

"Well, let's look over the ads while we get something to eat. I'm starving after last night. You know the best thing for the day after a binge." She grinned mischievously at me. "Biscuits and gravy."

I groaned. "I have a ton of work."

She stood and pulled on my arm. "Come on. I'm not letting you hide in here and stew. You and I are going to get some food and have some fun."

I let her pull me to my feet. This was the Becca I remembered. She never let me give up. Her talks helped me keep the nerve to stay at school and not transfer out junior year. "Okay, okay. Let me at least change out of my pajamas."

"Hurry," she said as I walked to the bedroom. "You know how vodka makes me crave carbs."

"If I remember right, it also makes your clothes fall right off," I called over my shoulder.

"Well, that too, but it wasn't until after we got home from the party." I heard the smile in her voice.

I tugged on a T-shirt and jeans. "Such restraint. You're so mature now." It felt good to joke. Forget Max. No more letting guys ruin my good times. "I'll bring my laptop so we can look at listings for apartments."

"You know, Max is going to need a roommate."

I yanked open the door from the bedroom and glared.

"Too soon?" she asked and shook her head. "You have to learn to laugh this stuff off. It's not worth your energy to stay angry."

Forcing a breath from my lungs, I imagined the bad emotions leaving my body with my breath like all those fancy meditation apps told you to do. "Well, he might have some cute firefighter friends."

"That's the spirit." She hooked her arm in mine as we headed for the door. "We'll find you an amazing apartment, and someday soon you'll meet an amazing guy like Brad, and then I can be your maid of honor."

If only it were that easy.

CHAPTER 11

MAX

I TOSSED THE CAN INTO THE RECYCLING WITH MORE FORCE THAN absolutely necessary. Even though my body was screaming with exhaustion, I barely slept at all after the bachelor party. Usually, no matter what was going on in my life, I could shut it off and go to sleep when I needed to. The one exception had been losing my grandparents. But stuff with women never kept me up at night.

Of course, I wasn't usually a large-scale ass to someone who, as it turned out, was the perfectly nice person she'd seemed to be. More than nice. She was great. And I'd messed it up.

"Hey, what did that soup can ever do to you?" Brad asked from the living room. "I was thinking we order pizza for dinner."

"I didn't hear you come in," I said. He'd stayed at Becca's place after the party. "Was everything okay after I left? I hope I didn't screw up the entire celebration." I'd followed Cassi out of the club, but not to try and talk to her. I watched from inside the glass door to make sure she got a ride. After she left, I didn't have the gumption to go back inside and face the mess I'd made, so I went home.

At least I'd been smart enough to stick to water all night.

Dealing with a hangover would have been the cherry on top of this sundae of crap that I'd created.

"It was a great party." Brad clapped me on the back. "Don't worry about anything, man. I know how much that watch means to you and thinking Cassi was Caroline, I can see how you thought she took it." He couldn't hide a smile. "Now I get why you were so pissed that I set you up with her."

"I really screwed up." I sat in my chair and stared at the garish Christmas tree. Maybe some time alone on Christmas will be good for me. And maybe I should make some of Gram's cookies. Her recipe book sat alone in the cupboard above the stove. I hadn't gotten it out once since she passed. I shuddered to think about what my grandparents would have thought about my behavior.

"Give her some time." Brad filled a glass of water. "Maybe Becca can smooth things over a bit. She was over there this afternoon to check on Cassi."

I waved off his concern. "Not a big deal. I'm just glad you guys enjoyed yourselves."

"Any luck on the roommate hunt?" he asked.

"Well, Francisco is looking for a place, but he snores loud enough to make the neighbors complain. And Jimmy had a friend who might be interested, but I've never met the guy." The idea of going from living with my oldest friend to a stranger was less than exciting. But plenty of people in Denver had roommates they didn't know well. I shook my head and changed the subject. "Less than a week and you'll be a married man."

The look that crossed over his face stopped my self-pity train. It was abject fear. Not the excitement you'd hope to see from an expectant groom. The expression was gone in a flash and replaced by a smile.

"You good, man?" I asked.

"Yeah, just pre-wedding nerves." He brushed off my concern.

"I'd never try to tell you what to do, but you know you don't have to go through with this, right?"

He sat on the couch and rested his head on the back. "I know. I almost told Becca I thought we should wait."

"Why didn't you?"

"She's so excited. It makes me feel so happy when I make her happy." He pressed his palms into his temples then let out a gale force breath. "I know she loves me. And she makes me feel so good when I'm with her."

"If there's one thing Grams and Pop taught me, it's that it takes selflessness and caring to make a marriage work. I just want you to be sure this is what you want, and not just what Becca wants." I leaned forward. "No judgement, man. I see the way she looks at you. I know she cares about you. But is she the one you want to be with forever?"

His hands fell to his sides. "When we're together, I'm sure."

A distinctive knock jerked our attention to the door. He shook his head and straightened. "Ah, never mind me. I've just got cold feet. It's all good."

From the knock, I knew who stood on the other side before I opened the door. "Hey, Becca." I stepped to the side. "Come on in."

She carried flattened cardboard boxes at her side as she walked in and spotted Brad. "There's my hubby-to-be."

"Let me help you with those, Babe." Brad jumped up from the couch.

She handed over the boxes and kissed his cheek. "I know I only left you a few hours ago, but I missed you."

"Did you check in on Cassi?" Brad asked.

I paused on my way to my bedroom to hear the answer.

"She'll be fine," Becca replied. "I got her out of her apartment and she cheered right up."

"That's great, Babe." Brad glanced my way.

Becca turned and faced me. "But I wouldn't recommend ever

talking to her again, Max." She put a hand on her hip. "I mean, not a single word. She doesn't want to see you ever. She'll put up with it at the wedding, for me, but just steer clear."

Barbed wire wrapped around my gut and tightened. I'd seriously messed up. "I really need to apologize to her."

"No." Becca held up a hand. "She'd appreciate it if you left her alone."

I straightened and nodded. It went against everything I'd been raised to do, not to take responsibility for my mistake and make it right. But if Cassi really didn't want to have anything to do with me, I had to respect her wishes. No matter how much I wanted to talk to her. To straighten things out. To tell her how sorry I was for behaving like an ass.

Becca shifted her attention to Brad, who was staring with wide eyes. "I decided since today is the only day we really have, we'd better get you packed up."

"Now?" he asked. "I figured we'd worry about that after the wedding."

I wanted to say something but bit my tongue. It wasn't my place. Seeing the moving boxes made this entire nightmare real. My best friend was moving out for good.

"But, Babe," Becca said. "Wouldn't it be nice to come home to our place as a married couple? We'll be in Cancun until New Year's and then it's back to work and the grind."

Brad shot me a deer in the headlights look. "I don't have anything ready."

"Plus," Becca said, as if Brad hadn't spoken. "Today we have Max and his muscles to help us." She sent me a smile. "Might as well put those bad boys to use, right?"

Brad caved. Like he always did. "Of course, you're right. I wasn't thinking about how much we'll have to do after the honeymoon."

So much for a nap.

~

I PUNCHED ANOTHER BUTTON TO CHANGE THE RADIO STATION. *Little Drummer Boy* rang out from the speakers. Gram's favorite Christmas song. My throat tightened with the hurt of missing her. She'd made the house cheerful with her cookies and her singing and her warmth.

"I miss your molasses cookies, Gram," I said out loud. With Brad moved out, I'd taken to talking to my grandparents to stave off the loneliness. "And you would have known what to do about this whole Cassi mess."

In the last few days, it seemed every station was giving in to the Christmas cheer. I made it halfway through the song before I smacked the knob to turn the radio off and drove in silence. The church was only a few minutes farther down the road, anyway.

Against Becca's advice, I texted Cassi an apology after one phone call that went straight to voicemail. The text went unanswered as well. But at least I'd apologized, both on her voicemail and in the text. I'd meant every word. I could admit when I was wrong, and boy, had I been. Our kiss under the mistletoe played through my mind for the thousandth time.

If I'd been paying attention, I'd have put together that her brothers were in the trades, which aren't typical professions for people who grew up with money. It should have been a clue, but I hadn't been truly listening.

I smacked the steering wheel of the truck and beat myself up some more. Even the guys at the station had noticed I was off. They refused to let me trade for a shift on Christmas. So, it looked like I'd be alone in my misery for the next few days.

Pulling into the church parking lot, I found an empty spot away from the life-sized nativity scene and took a moment to get into the right frame of mind. This was Brad's big day, or Becca's really. No reason to share my bad mood and ruin it for them.

I headed for the side entrance. Though I'd tried to resign

myself to letting Cassi be, part of me hoped I'd have a chance to apologize in person. Not to convince her to go out with me—she'd been through enough—but to show her I meant what I said.

A warm blast of air, heavy with the scent of pine and cinnamon spice, washed over me as I stepped inside. Brad had texted me that the groomsmen were getting ready in a room on the south side of the church and the bridesmaids were on the north side. I headed to the left and followed the sound of male voices and raunchy jokes. When I walked through the door, I spotted Brad immediately in the group of guys. He was pale to the point of his skin being translucent, and he looked like he was about to pass out.

CHAPTER 12

CASSI

"Has anyone seen my veil?" Becca called from behind the changing screen. "I think I might have left it at the apartment."

I flipped through the many garment bags hanging on the rod, three of which were Becca's. She wanted to change into two other dresses at the reception. I swore if I ever did get married, which was about as likely as getting struck by lightning in a snowstorm at this point, I'd have a simple ceremony. Maybe even elope to Vegas.

"Got it," I said.

She appeared from behind the screen, dressed in a silk robe with Bride embroidered on the front. "Oh, good. I was afraid I'd have to send you back to get it." Large curlers surrounded her head in a crazy-looking helmet. "Has anyone seen my parents yet?"

"Mom said the flight was delayed," Hannah piped up. "But they should get here before the ceremony."

Becca rubbed her temples, then refocused like a bulldog. "Cassi, get in this chair. It's time to make you beautiful."

The hair and makeup team had been working on Hannah, who rose from the seat, all painted and styled.

"Wow, Hannah," I said. "You look amazing." Her hair was curled and pulled into an up-do with swirling strands cascading down and a specially made holly leaf and berry accent on one side.

She grinned and ducked her head. "If only I had help like this every day."

"Where is Mercy?" Becca fumed.

We'd all been asked, more like ordered, to be at the church four hours before the wedding. A bit much, if you asked me, but Becca hadn't asked. "I'm sure she'll get here. We have two hours before the ceremony."

Becca pursed her lips. In the last few days, she'd gotten progressively more irritable.

"You need to sit down and get your makeup done." I pointed to the other chair. "There'll be plenty of time once Mercy gets here." I slipped my phone from my robe pocket and texted Mercy a nine-one-one.

She immediately answered with a thumbs up.

"Try to hold still so we get this right," the makeup artist said as she got to work.

I started to nod. "Oh, sorry."

Becca barked orders at Hannah and her other two brides-maids—people she'd met in law school who I'd never met before today. I tuned her out and focused on relaxing. I'd see Max at the altar. Then at the reception. Becca expected the traditional speeches. But after today I wouldn't have to see him again.

His voice from his message—so apologetic and full of regret—played through my head. He'd sounded so sincere, so sad at how he'd behaved. If I didn't know the truth about his lies after I'd left the bachelorette party, I'd have considered forgiving him.

I pushed the thoughts away. Having just gotten rid of one, the last thing I needed was another lying man in my life. No, Max and I weren't going to be a thing, no matter how amazing it felt when he'd kissed me.

"Hello." Becca snapped her fingers and met my gaze in the mirror. "What are you thinking about?"

I blinked. "Nothing."

"Right, I know that look." She scrunched her lips and nose. "He's not worth your time."

"I know." I glanced away. Mercy opened the door and slipped inside. I tried to distract Becca from noticing. "So, are you excited for the honeymoon?"

"Mercy." Becca spotted her late bridesmaid. "Where have you been?"

Mercy sighed and set her dress and a bag on a chair. "I had to run some Christmas cookies over to friends and family for my mom."

Becca crossed her arms. "Well, you're going to have to be last for the makeup and you better get started on your hair."

"I got here as quickly as I could." Mercy waddled to the chair to get her hair done. "But with the snow getting worse, it's sticking to the roads."

Becca glanced out the window at the heavily falling snow. "No! It can't be getting worse. What if people can't get to the church? Or the reception?"

"It's only supposed to snow eight inches. I'm sure they have the plows out," I reassured her. What do you expect this time of year?

"You're right." She slumped in her chair. "It'll be fine. Everything will be fine."

With an hour to spare, hair and makeup for the entire bridal party was done. "See?" I handed out glasses of champagne and a sparkling cider for Mercy. "We have plenty of time."

Becca downed her glass and poured some more. Her hands were shaking. "Oh my God, I'm getting married in an hour?"

I gripped her arm. "Hey, don't tell me that nerves are getting to the unshakable Rebecca Fernley."

She straightened and sniffed. "Of course not." She glanced at the still falling snow outside. "I just want to be sure this all goes off without a problem."

Mercy adjusted the strap on her curtain of a dress. The bodice fit to the empire waist then the fabric fell over her bigger-by-the-day belly in a red waterfall of chiffon. "I can go make sure the decorations and everything are set and see if guests are arriving."

Already in my own red nightmare of a dress, I jumped at the chance to get away for a bit. "I'll help. And I'll be on the lookout for your parents. Then you can rest assured everything is going as planned."

Becca nodded as she finished her third glass of champagne. I closed the door behind Mercy and leaned against it. "This can't be over soon enough."

"I don't know. You look pretty sexy in that dress, like a Christmas devil." Mercy winked.

"Right? This color is just not attractive."

We walked down the hallway to the chapel to check the decorations. I adjusted my stride for the four-inch red heels, impressed Mercy could pull off walking in them in her condition. The church had put out poinsettia arrangements and candles as well as red bows on each pew and white twinkling lights as a backdrop. It really was beautiful.

"I was actually supposed to be at my in-laws tonight. But Becca was in my wedding last year, so it's not like I could say no," Mercy said.

"I'm sorry I couldn't make it back for your wedding," I said.

"Don't be. You were in the middle of that awful breakup. Besides, I was the one who lost touch after I transferred schools." Mercy waved me off. "You can make it up to me and come to the baby shower next month."

I turned and spotted two men walking by the entrance to the chapel. My stomach dropped through the floor as recognition sparked and horrendous memories flooded my mind. Two of my worst tormentors from college were in the church. Tremors erupted in my hands and spread over my body like a tsunami. I leaned against the wooden pew for support. How could Becca have invited them? And not even warned me?

"Are you okay?" Mercy's gaze followed mine, and she stepped closer. "You look like you're going to fall over."

"It's nothing." I tried to paste a smile on my face, but it slid right off. "I just wasn't expecting to see them here."

Mercy frowned. "Becca invited a lot of friends from back in the day."

"They weren't friends after, well, that night," I said. Mercy had been there at the beginning of the night, before I'd decided it was a great idea to go skinny-dipping.

"What do you mean?" she pressed.

"They called me the Swan Princess for two years. They even asked if I gave private performances and all kinds of other disgusting things." I shook my head. "I can't believe she invited them."

"What?" Mercy paused, a confused expression on her face. "I wondered about this after the comment Becca made at the bachelorette party. That's why I asked you out to lunch."

"You wondered about what?"

"I thought the investigation was cleared up after Becca testified. How did the story even get around?" Mercy asked.

I stared at her. "Becca didn't testify. The investigation went all summer and into the next school year. Not to mention the divorce."

She rolled her tongue over her teeth. "She hung you out to dry?"

"What are you talking about?"

"Cassi, it was Becca's idea to go to the dean's house. I was there. I took off early because I still had some packing to do. Then she showed up back at the apartment in the morning without you, all drunk, laughing about how she took your clothes and left you on the swan. I went back, but you weren't there." Her eyes held a mountain of remorse. "I had no idea you were inside and the trouble you were in. I had to leave so I wouldn't miss my flight."

We'd been having a goodbye party for Mercy. With everything that happened after, I'd completely forgotten how the night started. I couldn't talk. Words refused to form in my stunned brain.

"I was in San Diego by the time I heard about the investigation, and I offered to come back and help clear everything up, but Becca said she was testifying, and it was no big deal."

No big deal. The exact words she'd said to me. To my face. "People tormented me for two years. Every time it came up, she told me it was my idea to go to the pool." Anger heated my skin to the point the snow would have sizzled off. I'd always wondered what I'd done with my clothes. "She never told you the mess I was in?"

"I swear." She shook her head. "If I'd known, I would have come back right away. But I suck at keeping in touch and she told me it was all fine."

The large room, with its cathedral ceilings, felt like it was caving in on me. "I need air."

She took my wrists. "Breathe with me. Deep breath in, and hold it, and blow it out." Mercy met my frantic gaze. "Again, you can do it."

I stood there and matched my breathing with hers until the walls stopped crushing me. "That's better. Thank you."

"Birthing class to the rescue." She released my hands. "Feel better?"

"Yes." I ripped the holly accent out of my hair and tossed it onto the floor. "But I'm done with Becca."

~

MERCY DIDN'T TRY TO TALK ME OUT OF IT OR STOP ME. SHE followed silently behind me in solidarity. I threw open the door to the dressing room, my jaw clenched so hard my teeth might crack. All these years. All the tears I cried, and she never told me the truth.

Becca stood in front of the mirror in her wedding dress. "Good, you're back. Grab my veil, will you?"

"No," I said and glared.

She turned at the tone of my voice. "What's going on?"

"Mercy was kind enough to fill me in on what actually happened that night at the dean's pool." For the first time in my life, punching someone sounded like a great idea.

"Mercy!" Becca gasped. Her face paled even under the layers of makeup. "Why would you bring that awful night up?"

"Don't turn this on her. She told me the truth. How you left me there, naked, and took my clothes." My voice rose with each word. "I could have drowned. So many times, I wished I had, instead of hearing all the slut comments, all the people calling me the Swan Princess." I held up a hand when she opened her mouth. "You blamed it all on me. You lied." I was shouting now. Everyone in the room watched us like we were in a morbid movie. "Why? Why did you keep convincing me to stay when you knew how terrible it was?"

"I couldn't lose you, too. It was just supposed to be a joke. I was so drunk I hardly remember doing it." A tear rolled down her cheek. "Mercy left, and it was just the two of us. I knew if you found out, you'd hate me. And you'd leave school. Besides," she said, going for her joking tone, "it's not like the dean was some old nasty guy. He was hot. Any girl on campus probably would have done him."

"That just made it worse because it was believable. You could have stopped it. Just by telling the truth. They didn't believe me because I couldn't remember how I got there, and you said I went alone." I stared at her in complete disgust, feeling like I was truly seeing her for the first time. Under all her bravado and sarcasm was an insecure little girl. A thought struck me. "What else have you lied about?"

"Nothing." She took a step toward me and held my gaze and tilted her head to the side just a touch. "I swear."

It was exactly the expression she'd used so many times over the years while she was spouting what I now knew to be lies. There's something else. Then it hit me. "Max wasn't drinking the night of the party. He never said anything bad about me, did he?"

"He left right after you did," Mercy put in.

Becca swallowed. "I didn't want you to talk to him anymore. Max might have known what actually happened in college. I told Brad the real story because I really do tell him everything. And I've been carrying this guilt around with me for six years," she said, as if I was supposed to feel sorry for her. "It killed me every time you were upset."

Mercy snorted from beside me.

"I was afraid Brad might have told Max the entire story. So, Max could have told you. I never considered the possibility until this whole mess started with him thinking you were Caroline, or I'd never have set you up with him. But I couldn't risk losing you right when I just got you back." Becca held out her hands to me.

I ignored the gesture. "You lied again. Just to suit yourself." I shook my head and grabbed my purse. "I'm done. Have a fabulous wedding. I never want to see you again."

"Cassi, please forgive me." Becca rushed toward me, but I backed away.

"Not a chance."

"You can't leave. You're my maid of honor," Becca called.

"Not anymore." I stormed from the room. Then the tears hit.

CHAPTER 13

MAX

Outside the dressing room, I paced, seriously wondering if Brad was going to make it through the ceremony without passing out. I considered going to the north dressing room to check on things and see if Cassi would give me the time of day. I started down the hallway but turned around at the halfway point. Better to wait until after the wedding.

"Max."

I recognized Cassi's voice immediately, and something was wrong. I spun around. She was in a bright red dress and heels. Even in the gaudy outfit, she looked amazing. Then I saw the tears. She wiped at her cheeks, and I rushed forward, digging my handkerchief from the inside pocket of the tux.

"Do you always carry one of those for damsels in distress?" She tried to laugh, but it came out choked. She took the white square and dabbed at her eyes.

"I would say that's what a gentleman does, but I've hardly acted like one." I stepped back to give her some space. "Are you okay?" Geez, moron, does she look okay?

She shook her head. "You know that story I told you about what happened in college?"

I frowned but nodded.

"Turns out Becca was behind the entire thing, and she let me take the fall." She pursed her lips as if tasting something sour. "Not only that. She lied and told me you were bad-mouthing me after I left the party." She glanced up to meet my gaze. "I wanted to tell you I don't blame you for how you acted. Caroline was awful. And with the silverware falling in my purse—"

"No," I interrupted her. I needed to get a genuine apology out. "I went into that restaurant with an idea in my head and even though you were sweet and amazing and funny, I didn't give you a chance." I wanted so much to pull her into my arms but held back. "I didn't really listen to what I was feeling. Talking to you was so easy. I haven't told anyone how hard it is with my grandparents gone. And when..." I almost said I kissed you but stopped myself and cleared my throat. "When I realized how much I'd hurt you..." My gaze dropped to the floor. "I understand if you don't want to see me again. But I want you to know how sorry I am."

She pressed her hand to my cheek until I met her gaze. "I forgive you."

It felt like aloe soothing a burn as relief cooled the shame I'd felt since the party. Before I could say anything, two guys in suits rounded the corner into the hallway. Cassi glanced over her shoulder then jerked back toward me, her face a mask of panic and her breath shallow.

"Hey, is that you, Cassi?" one guy called.

Cassi's head dropped.

"Holy crap. When did you get back in town?" the other one asked.

The distress in Cassi's expression left me seeing nothing but red. I stepped neatly around her and strode toward the two.

"You know, I have a pool now if—" the first one started, then his gaze settled on me.

"Go ahead," I practically growled. "Finish what you were

about to say." I leaned into the shorter men's space and hoped they would say just one more thing.

"Max." Cassi grabbed one of my arms. "Just ignore them."

"Hey, we were just saying hi to an old friend," the first said. "What's your problem?"

"Friend?" Cassi gasped. "We stopped being friends junior year."

"I was just joking about the pool." He moved to touch Cassi's arm.

I shook my head slowly as I straightened to my full height. His hand froze in air and both their eyes widened. "You both are going to apologize to this lovely woman right now."

"Max, they're not worth it." Cassi tugged on my arm.

"We're sorry," the first one stumbled over his words. "Just joking around."

"Yeah," the other stammered. "Just an old joke."

"Do I look like I'm laughing?" I wanted to break them over my knee like toothpicks, but I restrained myself. "Now apologize for how you treated her in college. And make it sound like you mean it."

"Okay, sure." They backed up a step. "We're sorry. We didn't mean anything by it." He looked past me to Cassi. "Everyone knew you didn't sleep with the dean. We figured you knew that."

A sigh escaped Cassi's lips and I turned my attention to her. She wasn't crying anymore. She stood with her back straight as a two by four and stepped in front of me. "You both tormented me. Along with half the school. If you see me on the street, walk the other way. If we run into each other in a store, you don't know me. We're not friends."

The two guys wilted. "Got it. Whatever you say." They spun and retreated down the hallway, but one stopped and looked back. "Cassi, I'm sorry. I really am."

She lifted her chin until they disappeared around the corner.

When they were out of sight, her shoulders slumped. "You didn't have to do that."

I slipped my arm around her. She didn't step away, but leaned into me. "Are you kidding?" I said. "That was the most fun I've had all week. Bullies aren't so tough when they're faced with someone a little bigger than them."

"A little bigger?" she laughed and snorted. "Do you not own a mirror?"

"Cassi?" Becca ran down the hallway, barefoot. "Cassi, thank God you haven't left yet. Please, let me explain."

Cassi spun on her heel and headed for a door to the parking lot. When I turned, I saw Brad had come out of the dressing room and was watching us. I strode toward him. "I've kept my mouth shut so far," I said. "But I have to ask. Are you sure you want to go through with this?"

He nodded.

I sighed. "You need to talk to Becca. Some stuff happened."

He clapped me on the shoulder. "I kind of gathered that."

I glanced out the windows at the snow-covered parking lot. "Sorry, man. I gotta go."

Disappointment showed in Brad's frown, but he nodded. "Don't worry about me. You go after Cassi."

I chanced a glance back at Becca and restrained myself from telling her exactly what I thought of her. With a shake of my head, I walked out the door. "Cassi," I called and jogged toward her car as she pulled out of her parking place. "Cassi, wait!"

She shook her head as she drove past me and turned out of the parking lot.

CHAPTER 14

CASSI

I took a small glass bulb out of the new package and hung it on the thin branch of the tree. The gas station hadn't had the best selection, but it was the only place open on Christmas day. Green tractors on the bulb, decorated in glitter, shimmered in the firelight.

The branch bent under the weight. The little tree had been all alone outside the closed Christmas tree lot, with a FREE sign on it. I couldn't leave without it.

I sat back and examined my work. An interesting combination theme of farm equipment and fifties memorabilia. A sad smile crept over my lips.

I'd talked to my oldest brother first thing in the morning. His four kids and wife all joined the video chat. Each of my nieces and nephews told me what Santa brought them. The loud ruckus reminded me of all the Christmases of our childhood. In the end, my brother tried to convince me to fly out tomorrow to visit them and stay through New Year's. Though the thought of being surrounded by rambunctious kids and holiday cheer was tempting, I couldn't bring my messed-up life to their happy house.

No, I'd stay here, in my apartment and deal with the fact that another person who I'd trusted was lying to me for most of our relationship. Two complete betrayals in two years. I was on a roll.

Becca's treachery left me in complete shock at first, but as my brain melted from its frozen state, so many pieces fell into place. So many little things she'd said to steer me in the direction she'd wanted now made sense because I understood her motivation.

I'd blocked her number after she'd called and texted multiple times before I'd even made it home from the church. A clean break was the best way to end a toxic relationship. That's what she'd told me when I'd left New York.

A knock at the door jerked me from contemplating the state of my life. I stiffened, then crept to the door without making any noise to peer through the peephole. Max stood in the hallway, only the bottom half of his face visible, but I'd recognize that chest and chin anywhere.

My heartrate sped up to a hummingbird's pace.

"Cassi?" he called through the door. "I just want to talk to you for a minute."

I glanced down at my sweatpants and T-shirt, then smoothed my crinkly hair. The hairspray and foam left it in stiff tangles when I'd yanked out the multitude of pins and stupid holly accent. I'd tried a messy bun, but the stiff hair pulled and added to my aching head. A shower was beyond my caring or energy at this point. At least I'd scrubbed all the makeup, ruined from crying, off my face before I fell into my bed.

Turning the bolt, I opened the door. "Hey."

He stood with his hands behind his back. His gaze took in every detail of me, from my socked feet to my crazy hair. "Are you holding up okay?"

I waved to my quirky tree. "I decorated and I've got a fire going. What more could a girl ask for?"

"A lot," he whispered.

His tone made me want to throw myself into his powerful arms, just for a minute. Just to not feel so alone.

But even as the thought crossed my mind, I knew I was lying to myself. I'd wanted to be in Max's arms ever since the kiss under the mistletoe. Maybe before.

"Mercy said the wedding went fine, besides Becca's parents not making it to the ceremony. They're off on their honeymoon," I said to fill the silence. "She's taking bets on the marriage not lasting six months."

"Let's not talk about them." He cleared his throat as if gearing up to say something. "I understand if you want to be alone with everything that's happened. But I have one question to ask."

I met his gaze and waited.

"Can we just start over? No pressure. Just you and me seeing where this thing between us goes."

One side of my mouth quirked up. He felt it too. I held out my hand.

His gaze darted to my extended hand, and I raised my eyebrows. He pulled one arm from behind his back but left the other. His large hand enclosed my own and his skin warmed mine.

"It's so nice to meet you." Something as tender as butterfly wings tickled my insides. "I'm Cassandra. But my friends call me Cassi."

A huge grin cracked his serious expression, and his dimple appeared. "I'm pleased to meet you, Cassi. I'm Maximillian. But my friends call me Max."

I gasped out a laugh. "Maximillian? Really?"

He shrugged. "Family name."

He didn't let go of my hand. His thumb traced very distracting circles over my skin. I pointed my chin to his other arm, which was obviously holding something behind his back. "What have you got there?"

"Remember how you said I should make a batch of my Gram's cookies?" he said as he pulled a covered plate into view. "And share them with someone special?"

The sting of tears pricked my eyes, but I blinked them away.

A tremor shook his voice. "Well, I can't think of anyone as special as you or anyone I'd rather share these with." He cleared his throat. "If you're up for it."

"I'd love to." Without thinking, I dropped his hand and stepped forward to wrap my arms around him. I looked up into his surprised face. I slowly stretched on my tiptoes, holding his gaze the entire time, until our lips met, and I closed my eyes. Just like our first kiss, electric tingles raced over my body like I'd never felt before.

His scent, clean and woodsy, now with a hint of molasses and sugar, enveloped me. His arm pulled me tight against his chest and my toes left the floor. In two steps he crossed the space to the kitchen counter and the plate clattered to the surface.

Both his arms held me, firmly but with tenderness. I moved my grip to around his neck and wove my fingers in his hair. The hurt and anger of the last week melted away. I'd never felt so safe, so cared for, in all my life.

We broke the kiss, both breathless.

"Wow," Max gasped.

"I… have cocoa," I stammered. "For the cookies."

Every part of the front of my body pressed against his muscled form. He held me for another few seconds, then lowered me so I was standing again but kept his hands on my hips. "Cocoa would be perfect."

ONE YEAR LATER

A FEW DAYS BEFORE CHRISTMAS

CHAPTER 15

CASSI

"Yum," I groaned and chewed a bite of the Cool Cucumber, my new favorite sandwich at the Italian Deli. The last few weeks, my stomach couldn't handle the spicy meats on the Mobster of Godfather.

"I'm glad to see you hungry again," Max said after swallowing his own bite. "That stomach bug did a number on you."

I nodded and busied myself with my pickle.

"So," Nate said as he approached the table. "How's my favorite couple? No Brad and Hannah today?"

Not only had the marriage not made it to six months, Brad and Hannah surprised everyone by starting to date a few months ago. With Hannah being more mature than her sister, the six-year age gap between her and Brad wasn't noticeable. They usually accompanied us to the deli. I'd never seen Hannah so happy or confident. "They left on a Christmas ski vacation to avoid family."

"I get it." Nate nodded. "Everything tasting okay?"

"It's amazing, as always," I said and wiped my mouth with the paper napkin.

"Hey," Nate exclaimed. "What's that I see?" He motioned to my hand.

I bit my lip and glanced at Max while I fiddled with the band of the ring—his grandmother's engagement ring. The swirls of the intricate filigree work in the platinum made the band sparkle almost as much as the center diamond. A moment of shock still washed over me every time the beautiful ring caught my eye.

"I somehow convinced her to keep me," Max said with a grin. His dimple that I loved so much appeared on his cheek.

"I have to ask" —Nate beamed and sent me a wink— "did he do a good job on the proposal? Because a girl like Cassi here deserves the best."

"He did a great job. He asked me to marry him over Thanksgiving weekend on a ski trip to Vail." I almost swooned at the memory—Max, down on one knee in front of a raging fire.

"Good man!" Nate rushed behind the counter and brought out two tiramisus, my favorite, and set them on the table. "This calls for a celebration. What are you going to do for Christmas to top that?" he asked Max.

I wasn't sure what Max had up his sleeve, but I was certain I could top it. My hand settled over my lower belly, and I thought of Max opening the Christmas gift I had wrapped and set under the tree. Keeping the baby a secret was killing me, but I wanted to surprise him and I hadn't wanted to say anything until the doctor confirmed the test results. Looked like we'd done more than just get engaged last month in Vail.

The bell over the door rang as a couple walked in. The man carried a toddler and held the door for the woman. The man glanced around the rows of red booths. Recognition set in. A fresh wave of nausea washed over me—so crippling that it felt like nails impaled my stomach.

Nate clapped Max on the shoulder and went back behind the counter.

I slid to the side and lay on the seat of the booth, hiding under the table. Please don't let him see me. Please.

CHAPTER 16

MAX

CASSI DROPPED LIKE A ROCK UNDER THE TABLE AND OUT OF SIGHT. I leaned to the side and twisted, trying to see her from my seat. My shoulders didn't want to fit, so I ended up laying on my back across the seat of the booth.

"What are we doing?" I asked. "Are you feeling sick again?"

"Please, just sit up and act like everything is normal," she whispered. "Pretend I'm not here."

"Your legs are sticking out of the booth." I frowned. "Tell me what's going on."

"I can't let him see me," she whispered.

"He, who?"

"Cassandra?" a male voice asked from beside the booth.

Cassi shot up in her seat. I finagled my way to a sitting position and narrowed my eyes at the man who obviously caused her distress. He'd left the toddler with the woman at the counter talking to Nate.

"Dean Warren," Cassi choked out. "I, um…"

Dean? As in that dean? I darted a look to Cassi's pale face and knew. Yep, that dean. My muscles tensed, ready to put a quick stop to this conversation if need be. I wasn't about to let this guy upset her anymore.

"I never got a chance to apologize—" Cassi began.

The dean held up his hand to stop her. "You actually did apologize. Many times. And in writing if I remember." He chuckled and smiled at her.

She swallowed. "I'm still so sorry."

"Don't be," he said. "That investigation and divorce were the best thing that ever happened to me." He glanced over his shoulder. "I wouldn't have met my wife. I wouldn't have taken a chance at a new job. I'd have been stuck in the same miserable place I'd been for years. So, thank you."

"I'm not sure what to say." Cassi shot a wide-eyed look my way. Her fear had given way to astonishment. I relaxed a bit.

"I'm the one who should be sorry. I can't imagine what you had to go through. Things worked out for me, but I always felt terrible about what you had to deal with. You handled yourself with grace and dignity that I admire but I never got a chance to tell you," the dean said and turned to me. "I'm sorry. I didn't introduce myself." He held out a hand. "Michael Warren."

"Max, Cassi's fiancé," I said and shook his hand.

"You've got a brave lady by your side. I wouldn't let her go if I were you."

"Don't plan on it," I answered. As he walked away, I reached across the table and took Cassi's shaking hand in mine. "Not ever."

PLEASE REVIEW

We hope you enjoyed *Merry Mix-Ups* by Emily Bybee. If you did, we would ask that you please rate and review this title. Every review helps our authors.

Rate and Review: Merry Mix-Ups

MEET THE AUTHOR

Emily grew up loving an escape to the fantasy world in books. While other kids were out and about, she loved hanging out at the library. Nothing made her feel as happy as walking out with a stack of books in her hands. At the age of twelve, Emily began writing after she had a series of extremely vivid dreams that begged to be made onto a story.

In high school and college, she focused on science and graduated with a degree in environmental biology with a heavy side of biochemistry. After college Emily began writing again, but quickly realized she had failed to take a single writing or grammar class. Luckily, she's a quick learner. She loves writing stories with interesting characters, from paranormal to suspense, but they all have to have a happily ever after.

www.ingramcontent.com/pod-product-compliance
Lightning Source LLC
Chambersburg PA
CBHW020544130626
46552CB00007B/2755